Mouth Open
Story
Jump
Out

GRACE HALLWORTH

Also by Grace Hallworth
Listen To This Story

for younger readers
Cric Crac

5

~~YARDLEY~~ WOO~~D~~

First published in Great Britain 1984
by Methuen Children's Books Ltd
Magnet paperback edition first published 1987
Published 1992 by Mammoth
an imprint of Reed Consumer Books Limited
Michelin House, 81 Fulham Road, London SW3 6RB
and Auckland, Melbourne, Singapore and Toronto

Reprinted 1994

ISBN 0 7497 1038 1

A CIP catalogue record for this title
is available from the British Library

Printed and bound in Great Britain
by Cox & Wyman Ltd, Reading, Berkshire

Contents

Introduction   *page 9*

1. The Soucouyant
   page 11

2. The Loup Garou
   page 23

3. La Diablesse
   page 33

4. L'Esprits
   page 47

5. Le Diable
   page 65

6. Douennes
   page 79

7. Papa Bois
   page 87

8. Fairymaids and Mermaids
   page 103

*To all
my friends and relatives
who told me stories*

Introduction

I remember a time when stories about supernatural beings were a strand in the web of stories which were told orally in Trinidad and Tobago. They were part of the normal exchange of news and events and were related as true happenings in which real persons played a role.

Perhaps the storyteller was walking along a dark quiet road one night and saw a ball of fire hovering in the sky ... or, perhaps the grandfather of another storyteller once met a beautiful woman at a dance in a village and she invited him to accompany her home as she was nervous of walking the dark streets. On their way he struck a match to light his pipe and in that instant he saw her face ...

Of course there are people who will deny that supernatural beings exist except in the imagination and will offer convincing explanations for the 'imagined' apparitions. They seldom shake the faith of those who believe that all things are possible in heaven and earth. Besides, what rational explanation can be offered for the incident in which a businessman is advised that his rival takes the form of a bat and that if he were wounded in this form he would cease to be a threat? The businessman follows instructions and wounds the bat in four places. Later that day his rival is taken to hospital with severe fractures in the four places corresponding to the bat's wounds!

As more and more people used electricity supernatural beings were exorcised from their favourite dark haunts. But they have not been completely routed, and there are a few which have no need of the mantle of darkness. Late one night when the moon is full you may find your path barred by a man whose legs are so long that they span the width of the street. As you look up you will see his body stretching up almost to the sky. Know then, that you have met the Moongazer and turn back before it is too late!

Supernatural beings still have a strong hold on our imaginations if not on our actual lives and among a group of West Indians in a relaxed atmosphere it is not difficult to start a chain of stories which strain and jostle to be told. Whether or not the storyteller believes in supernatural beings, or whether the storyteller is relating a personal experience, the stories have the power to thrill and entertain. I hope that these stories will do both, so MOUTH OPEN, STORY JUMP OUT.

1. The Soucouyant

The Soucouyant (Sukuya) is probably the best
known of all the supernatural beings and
whether she is called Old Hag, Old Higue, or
The Old Witch depends on the part of the
Caribbean from which the story originates.

She makes a pact with the devil - an
exchange of human souls for the power to
change herself into some other form. Then at
night she sheds her human skin and becomes a
ball of fire. In this form she flies about and
sucks the blood from human beings and animals
by puncturing their necks. Before the cock crows
and dawn breaks she must return inside her skin
or lose her power. Sometimes she takes the form
of an animal or may cast a spell on someone
who also becomes an animal . . .

A strange cat used to visit a bakery and spoil batches of freshly-baked bread. At first the baker set traps to catch the cat but when they proved useless he became suspicious. He noticed that the cat appeared at special times of the month and since he was a man who had knowledge of witch lore, he knew that he was not dealing with an ordinary animal. So he checked his calendar and made his plans.

One night he stripped off all his clothes, placed a wreath of leaves and straw on his head and waited near the oven. The strong yeasty smell of baking bread filled the air. There was a new moon and the baker was well-prepared.

At midnight the cat came hugging the wall and stepping cautiously. Occasionally it paused to look around and sniff the air before taking another step. It circled the wall twice before it ventured to cross the yard to the oven. Then as it approached and poised to leap on to the baking trays, the baker lunged at one of its legs with a sharply-pointed iron rod.

The cat screamed with pain and blood spurted from its wounded leg. The baker quickly turned on all the electric lights to see what was happening. He saw the cat trying to drag itself away from the light but something seemed to be holding it to the place where it was when the baker wounded it. The spell which the baker had made was so strong that the cat could not move until he removed the wreath from his head. When he did so the cat changed very slowly into an old woman, who was actually a neighbour of the baker.

When she was 'freed' she hurried home and took to her bed. Her shame was so great that she refused to see a doctor to treat her leg, which began to decay. Her health got worse and the neighbours called in the priest but she would not denounce the devil. So she died without the blessing of the Church and is said to roam the village in the form of a cat.

A Ball of Fire

Everyone knew that Nen Marie was a soucouyant. She was an old woman who lived in the ramshackle hut on the outskirts of the village with nothing but her cat for company.

Whenever she went into the village mothers made the sign of the cross as she passed and men shook their fists behind her back. If there were no grown-ups around, children ran after her shouting,

> 'Nen Marie you old souci'
> Nen Marie you can't catch me
> So go and suck a cow for tea.'

But just to be on the safe side every child wore a necklace of jumbie beads to ward off the evil eye of Nen Marie.

As far as anyone could remember Nen Marie had only been accused of the deaths of Farmer Meikle's cow and the shopkeeper's dog. The cow had chased her across a field, and the dog had barked at her heels as she left the shop one day so when they died soon after, the villagers said that Nen Marie had put mal y'eux, the evil eye on the animals.

Then in one week two mothers lost their babies.

People were convinced that Nen Marie put mal y'eux on the children because their mothers had not yet protected them with necklaces. The shopkeeper's wife began the rumour, 'The old witch had to lengthen her life so she steal the children's soul.' And a number of people swore that they saw a ball of fire near Nen Marie's hut late one night.

In the village feeling against Nen Marie was strong and bitter. It was so strong that word reached the priest that there was trouble afoot and he paid a special visit to the mothers who had lost their babies. He spoke about a welcome in heaven for the innocent children and the mothers listened in silence. Uneasy about the mood, he preached a sermon on Sunday about the sin of bearing false witness. The congregation wore a mask of indifference but decided in their hearts to seek help elsewhere. When they left the church all the pent-up anger of the past few weeks burst forth and one mother cried, 'How many innocent children have to die before the old witch get her come-uppance?'

The shopkeeper's wife said, 'When it come to mal y'eux and matters of that kind, the priest and them is no use. It is we who have to find our own salvation.'

They found a wise man or obeah man who agreed to come to the village but he said, 'I can't promise you anything until I see for meself, a skin without a body.' And he began to watch Nen Marie's hut at night.

Some time passed and then one day the obeah man met the villagers.

'There are signs and signs,' he said. 'And I think that by tomorrow morning we should have proof. Bring me a bag of salt, a bottle of holy water and a thick piece of wood from the poui tree.' Armed with all these things he took up his night watch near the old woman's hut.

At midnight he saw Nen Marie leave her house and head towards a small wooded area where she disappeared from sight. A few minutes later he saw a ball of fire shoot up from the copse and float away in the direction of the village centre. Quickly he ran along the path which led to the wood and began to search the area. Yes, there partly hidden in the undergrowth was a wooden mortar. In it was the evidence he sought – the skin of Nen Marie.

He emptied the bag of salt over the skin, which began to writhe in hideous contortions. When all movement ceased he turned the skin inside out using the poui stick, for he had to make sure that no part of the skin was left unsalted. Then he sprinkled the holy water around the mortar.

He had barely returned to his hiding-place when he saw the ball of fire. It hovered over the copse for a few seconds before descending. Slowly the man walked towards the spot. There was nothing to fear. The holy water would render the soucouyant harmless. There was no need for haste. The salt would render the skin useless. The soucouyant was entirely powerless.

He came on Nen Marie as she was struggling to get into her skin but it had shrunk so much that it would not fit her. She tried it this way and that, and as the brine burned her, she cried out in pain,

> 'Skin, skin you na know me?
> Skin, skin why you burn me?
> Skin fight with me, skin tight for me
> Skin, skin why you na go on me?'

16

It was no use. Gradually her struggles became weaker until all her life ebbed away. As the clouds of night parted to let the sun through, and the cock crowed, the obeah man went to the village. He brought the people to the place where the old woman lay with the shrunken skin beside her.

And ever since that day the people of that village will neither lend nor borrow a mortar. They say, 'It's not everyone who does use their mortar for pounding breadfruit!'

The Witch of Dennery

Ma Grimes lived in the village of Dennery in St Lucia. She was called La Sorcière: the witch.

Ma Grimes was so old that even grandparents remembered her as an old woman when they were children. They had been told to keep away from her and they told their children, who in turn told their children.

'Eh bien,' they whispered. 'She is older than the mountains beyond the village. She cheats death and that is wicked.'

But there was more to it than that. If the village folk trusted you they would tell you a story about Ma Grimes that everyone knew as well as they know the Lord's Prayer.

One day a visiting family arrived in Dennery. They went on a picnic in the forest which was beautiful at that time of year. They sent the two children, Elijah and Julie, to collect wood for a fire on which to cook the food they had brought. Julie wandered off and could not find her way back to the path. She came to the place where Ma Grimes lived in her little shack. There was plenty of wood stacked up around the shack so Julie thought, 'If I can get some pieces of wood here I shall be able to get back before Elijah.'

She knocked on the door.

When Ma Grimes opened the door and saw Julie, her eyes grew bright.

'Child, what are you doing out here all alone?' she asked.

'I was looking for wood for my parents,' replied Julie. 'But I lost my way. Would you give me some of your wood and show me how to find the path?'

'Yes, dearie,' said Ma Grimes. 'But you must be thirsty after such a long walk. Come in and have a cool drink before we set out.'

The old woman seemed so kind and harmless that Julie had no fear and she followed her into the shack. Quickly Ma Grimes went to her kitchen and mixed a potion which she gave to Julie to drink. No sooner had Julie done so than she changed into a big frog. The only thing about her which did not change were her large brown eyes which were flecked with grey.

Meanwhile Elijah had found some wood and returned to his parents.

'Where is Julie?' they asked.

They searched everywhere but Julie could not be found.

As night fell they went to the police station to get help but the chief constable was away, so they were taken to the headman of the village.

As soon as he heard their story he suspected that Julie had been stolen by Ma Grimes but he did not tell the parents his fears.

'Rest now and tomorrow we will find Julie,' he said.

So early next morning they set off for the forest. The headman took the path leading to Ma Grimes's shack.

As they were walking along a large frog leapt out from the bushes and stood in front of them. It looked up at the parents and kept opening and closing its mouth but no sound came from it.

Elijah, who was fond of animals, bent down to stroke the frog. Suddenly he stood up and said, 'Mama, Papa, look the frog has eyes just like Julie's.' His parents were angry with Elijah for they thought he was acting the fool when they were sick with worry. But the headman stooped down and picked up the frog. He looked at it carefully.

'We will take the frog with us,' he said. And when the parents asked him for a reason he would say no more.

At last they came to the shack where Ma Grimes lived. The headman drew a circle outside the shack and said to the others, 'Now I want you all to stay inside this circle. Whatever happens do not step out of it until I give you the word.'

They promised to do as he asked and he entered the shack.

Ma Grimes was quite surprised to see the headman. He was the one person in the village she feared for he was a good and wise man and they had met before.

'Ma Grimes,' said the headman. 'You know why I am here so let us not waste words and time. Tell me what to do to free the child from this hideous form?'

'Man,' replied Ma Grimes. 'Too often you set yourself against me but bambé yo' go see that my power is stronger.'

The headman's voice grew hard.

'Old woman,' he said. 'You may cheat death but

while I stay here your power will get weaker and I will not leave this hovel until the child be safe.'

Ma Grimes knew the headman's powers. He was well armed against her spells and designs. She could not harm his person but she might still defeat him by cunning.

'I set you a riddle,' she said. 'If you rightly answer I will free the child. Will you agree?'

The headman agreed willingly but he said, 'First you must swear by all your powers on this sacred bag that you will keep your promise.'

Ma Grimes looked into the bag and saw the unnameable relics. She trembled with fear and tried to get out of taking the oath but the headman would not yield. And so she swore. Then she set him this riddle:

'Green, green the blanket over me
Red, red the walls around me
No living human kind you'll find
Yet life thrives all about me.

Water, bone, dust and clay
All this will pass away
Breath and life still find shelter
In those things disguises alter.

What man scorns will shun the light
Gain its powers from the night
Earth to earth and dust to dust
Evil triumphs where it must.'

As the sun moved on its journey and the shadows began to appear on the walls of the shack the headman sat still and silent trying to work out the meaning of the riddle.

All of a sudden the frog, which he had put on the

floor, jumped on to his lap. He was about to push the ugly cold creature off when he remembered that it was really a little girl. At that moment everything was made clear to him. If what he thought was true then the old witch had not only set him a riddle, she had told him the secret of her power.

He began to speak words which were indeed the answer to the riddle and as he spoke she cringed. The look of fear in the old woman's eyes was sufficient proof for him.

'Now evil one,' the headman commanded. 'Release this child from the body of that creature and return her to human form.'

And so it was that Julie was returned to her parents, a lively little girl with large brown eyes flecked with grey.

But no one else knows the answer to the riddle except perhaps Julie. Do you?

2. The Loup Garou

The Loup Garou (Loogaroo), also called Ligahoo or Lagahoo, is a man who takes on the form of an animal to carry out his work for the devil at night. Although he is feared as a werewolf, he is often a highly respected member of the community and a powerful obeah man ...

The Stable-Owner

In a certain village a Loup Garou was taking so much blood from horses in their stables that they became weak and unable to work. The stable-owners could find no cause for the sudden epidemic but one man among them believed that there was more to it than met the eye. He decided to keep watch over his stable.

Night after night he kept vigil but saw nothing which seemed out of the ordinary. After two weeks of watching he was about to give up when he saw a donkey enter the stable one night. It was the strangest donkey he had ever seen for it was the size of an Alsatian dog covered with black bristly fur and its mouth was full of long pointed teeth.

The stable-owner watched as it made for a horse and fastened its teeth in the horse's neck. There was nothing he could do at the time because he had no protection against the creature. But early next morning he melted down some silver dollars and made a bullet and placed it in a gun. On that same night when the Loup Garou returned to the stable, the owner took careful aim and fired at the animal. The bullet caught the creature in one of its front legs and it leapt about four feet in the air and came down again and was through the stable-door in one bound.

The stable-owner followed a trail of blood which led to the house of a very important man in the village. 'Surely Mr De Groos would not be mixed up in witchcraft?' mused the stable-owner. But he could not doubt the evidence of his eyes. He decided to wait and find out what took place so he took up a position near the house where he could see without being seen.

Soon a car drew up and someone stepped out. It was the doctor. No sooner had he entered the house when an ambulance arrived and two attendants with a stretcher followed him into the house. A few seconds later they came out carrying Mr De Groos on the stretcher, got into the ambulance and quickly drove away. As soon as the coast was clear the stable-owner came out from his hiding – place and returned home.

Several days passed and there was not even a whisper of news about Mr De Groos. Was he alive or dead? If he was alive what had he said to his wife, or the doctor? These were some of the questions that troubled the stable-owner and he expected to find the police on his doorstep at any moment. Yet he held his peace and did not even confide in his wife.

One day a large black car stopped outside his house. He could not imagine who his wealthy visitor might be and then he saw a limping figure. It was Mr De Groos, the man he had shot. Shaking with fear, he opened the door and confronted his visitor.

'Whatever you plan to do, let it be between you and me, Mr De Groos. My wife don't know anything about what pass between us at the stable that night,' he whispered.

'Nor mine,' replied Mr De Groos. 'I told every one that I was cleaning my gun and it went off by mistake.'

'In that case why don't you let it go at that. I am willing to forget the matter if you are,' said the stable-owner.

'Indeed that's just what I want so let's shake on it,' said Mr De Groos and he clasped the stable-owner's hand leaving a silver bullet in it. 'I'll return what's yours at the same time,' he said smiling, and then he turned around and limped back to his car.

The stable-owner stood at his door with the silver bullet in his hand and a strange feeling came over him. He felt as though his whole body was covered with a rash. There was such a throbbing in his head that he felt it would burst open. He turned to face his wife who had come along to see who had called. She stepped back in surprise and then she said in a horrified whisper, 'Oh my God, Manfred, what happen to your face with all that hair on it. And yo' teeth, yo' teeth just like a lagahoo!'

The Headless Rider

A long way from the city there was a village which was said to be haunted by a creature so fearsome that anyone who saw it was struck dumb.

The villagers huddled inside their houses at night and even when the doors were bolted and the windows barred they did not feel safe. When they woke one morning and found several of their animals mauled about their necks, the villagers panicked.

They marched to the police station to make a complaint and demand action. One of the villagers had lost a thoroughbred horse and two bullocks and his blood was up. He appointed himself leader of the protest and spokesman, 'Matters gone too far now,' he said when they met the policeman. 'It's high time that you police went out and worked for your pay instead of hiding in here behind bars like prisoners. If you can't stop this creature then the Commissioner will have to find somebody who can.'

But the two policemen were local lads and determined to keep their distance from the creature. 'If you don't trouble jumbie, jumbie won't trouble you,' replied one of the policemen. And they refused to set foot outside the station after dark.

Soon word reached the Commissioner's ears that the two policemen were not patrolling the village at night because of their fear of the jumbie. 'It's a load of mumbo jumbo and hocus – pocus,' exploded the Commissioner. 'I will not have my rules broken by two cowardly and superstitious policemen.' And he immediately sent one of his best corporals to take charge of the village station. No sooner had the corporal arrived and begun his nightly patrol than he was rushed back to the city to hospital. A villager had found him wandering in the fields early one morning. His mind was in such a state of confusion that he could neither remember who he was nor where he was.

Policeman after policeman came and went in swift succession. They arrived hale and hearty and ready to tackle the jumbie but their stay was short and in the village the rumour was rife that each policeman was driven mad after a night patrol.

Meanwhile in the city, the Commissioner addressed his men, 'What kind of a police force is this?' he asked. 'It seems that we have here a nest of mice instead of a team of well-trained men. I shall have to go to the village and settle the matter myself.' At these words a young policeman called Dookie spoke, 'Sir,' he said. 'I believe that someone in the village is making monkeys of us. Let me go and prove to the villagers that this so-called jumbie is just flesh and blood like the rest of us.' Dookie was an ambitious young man, eager for honours and promotion.

Shortly after Dookie arrived in the village, Mr Harris, the wealthiest farmer in the district, visited him. He was a big man with a great deal of hair all over his body. When he walked his massive head hung down as though it were too heavy for the long neck. The strangest thing about him were his knees and the palms of his hands. The skin on them had been scraped away leaving the soft fleshy portions red and raw.

Mr Harris spoke about many things and as he was about to leave he said, 'Now, Constable Dookie, let me give you a piece of advice. We have a jumbie in this village that don't like policemen so if I were you I would stay indoors at night.'

'True, Mr Harris?' replied the constable. 'Well, let *me* tell you something. Just in case you meet this jumbie of yours, you tell it that Dookie ain't like the other policemen. Tell it from me that the spirit that could frighten me ain't dead yet.'

Mr Harris shook his head and said, 'You're a young man, Constable, and you have much to learn. Remember, what ain't meet you ain't pass you.' And with that warning he took his leave.

After the meeting, Constable Dookie was determined to prove that he was in command. Every night, as bold as brass, he rode his horse around the empty village and he met not a soul, neither living nor dead. Sometimes to liven things up he shouted,

'Jumbie, jumbie where you hiding?
I am Dookie. I'll be riding every night.
So jumbie, jumbie come and fight.'
29

Soon the children began to chant Dookie's challenge in the playground,

> 'Jumbie, jumbie where you hiding?
> I am Dookie. I'll be riding every night.
> So jumbie, jumbie come and fight.'

It wasn't long before everyone in the village knew it well. And not at all surprising that the calypsonians found a catchy tune to put to the words:

> 'Jumbie, jumbie where you hiding?
> I am Dookie and I'll be riding
> Every night, every night, every night
> So jumbie, jumbie come and fight.'

Of course no self-respecting jumbie would put up with this kind of ridicule for long. And besides Dookie used to shout his challenge right outside Mr Harris's house.

One night when Dookie was out on patrol he heard the sound of hooves coming in his direction.

'Strange!' he said to himself. 'I have been here for three months and never met another person out at night.' He was curious to see who it was that dared to break the self-imposed curfew of the villagers.

As the sound of hooves drew nearer, Dookie's horse began to act very strangely. It became restless, straining to turn around away from whatever was coming. While Dookie was trying to control the horse, he heard something else that set his heart pounding. It was the clanking of chains, clatank! clatank! against the surface of the road. Now, the horse was frantic. It was plunging and snorting so wildly that Dookie could barely stay in the saddle. He was about to give it its head when he saw coming towards him, a gigantic black

horse dragging heavy chains. Seated astride the horse
was a body without a head. From deep within the
belly of the horse came awful groans as though it were
in great anguish.

Dookie opened his mouth to scream but not a sound
escaped. Fear froze him to his horse and he sat like a
carved figure. It was just as well that the horse knew
the way home and needed no guidance. It turned and
bolted and never stopped until it arrived at the police
station. Were it not for the stamping and snorting of
the horse Dookie's colleagues would not have known
that he had arrived; for he could not move or speak
and was in a deep coma. The two policemen had to

lift him down from his horse and carry him into the station.

It was a full two weeks before Dookie was able to speak and relate what had happened that night. The first thing he did was to write a letter to the Commissioner of Police begging for a transfer back to the city at once.

3. La Diablesse

*La Diablesse (Lajables), or lady-devil is
another witch who usually travels at night. She
loves to dance and often appears at dances where
she tempts men and leads them astray so that
they are lost for days. Or, she may lead them to
their death unless they are lucky enough to spot
the cloven hoof beneath her long full skirt ...*

Deadly Beauty

One night a young woman appeared at a village dance. No one knew who she was and no matter how they questioned her she managed to avoid telling anything about herself. The women were immediately suspicious but the men, both young and old, flocked around her like bees drawn to honeysuckle.

A young man named Hugh arrived at the height of the dance and saw at once that the young woman was the centre of attraction. Now Hugh was known to be a lady-killer and his path through life was strewn with the broken hearts of his conquests, young girls who were foolish, or unfortunate enough to have fallen in love with him. He was handsome, charming and wealthy so it was not difficult for him to attract women, even those well aware of his reputation.

With all the confidence of one who was used to having his own way, Hugh approached the attractive girl and asked her for a dance.

'Sorry,' she said, 'but I've promised six dances already. If you like I'll keep the seventh one free.'

Hugh was taken aback. Perhaps the young woman did not know who he was, if she did she would know that he never asked for anything twice. He retreated to the bar to plan his strategy. After some discreet questioning he found out the names of the six men to whom the girl had promised dances. Not one of them was willing to yield his place to Hugh despite threats and offers of money. And it was not until near midnight that the seventh set began and he found the young woman standing before him.

It was Hugh's chance to get his own back and he wanted to turn and walk away from her but she was all smiles and sweet words. Her voice was as soft and gentle as a lullaby. He took her in his arms and began to dance with her as though he were under a spell. At the end of the dance he heard himself offering to take her home. She agreed and quickly, eagerly he left the dance hall with her and arm in arm they walked along the moonlit road.

He was so infatuated with her charm and wit that when she suggested that they leave the main road for a secluded path he did not think it strange that she should be so forward. She took the lead and he followed where she led for as long as he could see her. But then dark clouds hid the moon and she disappeared. Suddenly Hugh was enveloped in a strange blackness. It was odd, too, that he could not hear the woman's footsteps any longer.

Without light or sound he could not be sure of his ground. He stumbled over uneven mounds of earth and blundered into thorny bushes and trunks of trees. Suddenly he found himself climbing; he couldn't tell what was on either side of him. A curious sensation at the back of his neck warned him that something evil was close by. He stood still and called to his female companion but there was no sound and no reply. A sliver of moonlight pierced the clouds. Light! He remembered that he had a box of matches in his pocket. In the same instant that he struck a match he saw a large white hog with fiery eyes coming towards him.

Early next morning, a gardener on his way to an allotment found Hugh lying in a furrow on a steep hillside. His clothes were badly torn and his shoes were nowhere to be seen. One of his arms and several ribs were broken but he was alive. The gardener looked over the side of the hill and shuddered at what he saw. Had the furrow not broken Hugh's fall he would have rolled down a ravine and almost certainly been dashed to pieces on the large boulders below.

Please take my coat

Everyone in the village believed that to go out at night was like flying in the face of God. Everyone, that is, except Johnno, the village idiot. The villagers fretted and fumed about his behaviour, 'Ebe oui don don!' they exclaimed. 'But look how the boy vaunting himself at night with his coming and going at all hours. It is certain that he will meet a bad end.'

One night Johnno was returning from a religious ceremony and was caught in a heavy downpour of rain. He had taken a short cut across the fields and the path became so muddy that he took off his shoes. His bare feet sank deep in the red oozy earth until his legs, from toes to knees, were completely encased in mud. They looked deformed and monstrous.

As Johnno emerged from the fields he saw a woman standing in the middle of the road. She wore a red blouse and a long white skirt, and although it was still raining hard there was not a drop of water on her. Johnno was not a boy to thrust himself forward but he had a soft spot for the opposite sex. He approached the woman and said, 'Miss, the rain will spoil your lovely dress. Please take my coat.'

The woman smiled and took the coat from Johnno's hand and threw it over her blouse.

'How is it that you are out so late?' she asked.

37

'This ain't late,' replied Johnno. 'Often I walk this road two and three o'clock in the morning, and it's not even midnight as yet.'

'And nobody warn you about the strange characters you could meet at night?' she enquired.

'What about you?' countered Johnno. 'How is it that you ain't afraid of them?'

'Ah!' she says with a funny smile. 'What's tonic for the goose may be poison for the gander. Some of us can walk the road at any time of night.'

'The next thing you will tell me is that you are one of the night creatures that my mother is always warning me about, like Lajables with the cloven hoof,' said Johnno.

'Do you mean a hoof like this?' she asked and lifting her skirt she revealed a cloven hoof!

'Well,' says Johnno as cool as you please. 'I certainly don't mean hooves like these.' And he hitched up his trousers to reveal his grotesque legs.

The woman looked down and immediately let out a shriek loud enough to be heard at the farthest end of the village. Before Johnno could explain she was half running, half flying with the speed of a jet about to take to the air. Johnno stood in the middle of the road for a long time wondering what could have frightened the lovely lady so badly that she flew away but he could not think of a single thing. So he picked up his coat which she had dropped in her haste to escape, and went home.

The next morning when his mother was brushing mud off Johnno's clothes she saw the print of a little red hoof in the back of the coat. She questioned Johnno closely about it but he had completely forgotten the incident so she never discovered what had hap-

38

pened. And try as she might she never got rid of that hoof mark.

The torchlight which policemen carry on night patrol is probably the best weapon for dealing with Lajables who hate light. But who knows what may come in handy when dealing with the supernatural ...

The shiner

Late one night a policeman was riding home when he saw a young woman walking along a road. The policeman was young and eager for a bit of excitement. He was also a new recruit and did not have the experience which encourages caution, so he approached the woman.

'A young lady like you should not be out alone at this hour,' he said.

The woman appeared to be shy for she kept her face hidden and did not reply.

The policeman persisted. "Would you like a lift home on my bicycle?" he asked.

The woman continued walking and said nothing.

Her attitude made him more determined. 'Come now, lady,' he urged. 'Surely you don't believe I would harm you. Just tell me where you live and I will see you home safely.'

The woman stopped and shyly said, 'It's not far from here but if you insist I will go with you.'

She was hoisted on the crossbar and they set off pleasantly enough. The policeman was teasing and joking, and though the woman was laughing merrily she hardly said a word. They had not gone very far when the policeman found that he could not turn the pedals as easily as before, yet the road was quite flat. He thought to himself, 'She was as light as a bundle of feathers when we started off. Now she is a dead weight.' He began to feel uneasy as he remembered he had not seen her face.

'Lady, you didn't tell me where you live,' he said.

'Just a little way to go. Keep straight on,' she replied with a strange laugh.

After a few seconds passed with no more directions, he asked, 'Lady, how much further?'

Her reply was the same as before, 'Just a little way to go. Keep straight on.'

The policeman was labouring with the load he carried. He felt as though his lungs were bursting and fear seeped through every pore of his skin as he recalled that there were no houses ahead of them. He was heading for a part of the town where the only buildings were warehouses. Beyond them lay the open sea.

A number of small boats and trawlers were bobbing up and down in the harbour. A light from one of them shone on the silver buttons of the policeman's tunic which formed the pattern of a cross. The emblem of the Star of Bethlehem on his helmet glinted in the dark. He braked and was about to accuse the woman of making a fool of him when she leapt off the bicycle and turned to face him. As she did so she saw the two emblems. She screamed and hid her head in her hands but not before the policeman had seen eyes like burning coals in a corpse-like face. From her mouth burst flames of fire. He jumped on his bicycle and rode away as fast as his trembling legs could pedal, her shrill fiendish laughter pursuing him as he fled. The echo of her words rang in his head for several days, 'You lucky, you lucky to be wearing that uniform, or your soul would be mine tonight and your body food for the fish. You luckeeeeee. . . .'

Since that day the policeman has kept the buttons on his tunic and the badge on his helmet so well polished that he is known as 'The Shiner'.

The Intake

Constable St Clair had been stationed at a country outpost for just a year when he received orders to patrol the first six miles of mountain road leading up to a place where the river was dammed. This place was known locally as 'The Intake' and from there water was piped to the villages scattered along the sides of the mountain.

The Intake was an eerie place even in daytime. About a mile off the road, it was heavily shrouded with large trees. Long thick vines wove themselves around massive tree trunks, binding the trees together and creating a lattice-work screen and support for climbing plants, snakes and birds. It was also the haunt of Les Diablesses and the villagers gave the place a wide berth at night.

At ten-thirty that evening St Clair left the station with a heavy heart for he knew well the reputation of The Intake. St Clair was no hero but he wanted to keep his record clean. And like everyone else in the police force he had his eye on quick promotion. Also, he knew that the Superintendent was not above checking up on his men during the night patrol.

41

'Somehow or the other,' he argued with himself. 'I have to keep one eye out for the Super and the other eye out for Les Diablesses.'

St Clair arrived at the beginning of the mountain road and looked up as far as he could see. The moon shone brightly down on the road but off to the sides the trees grew thick and tall and it was impossible to see what lurked behind them. Back and forth, forth and back went the silent arguments in St Clair's head. Finally he said loud enough for any one who was nearby to hear, 'It's no use tempting fate and looking for trouble. If the Super come, well he come, but I don't intend going anywhere near that Intake tonight.' And having made his decision, he set out to patrol the road up to the three-mile post and not a foot further.

As he was climbing the road he heard voices. He stopped and listened carefully. From a distance they sounded like women's voices but he couldn't be sure. So he stood where he was and waited to see who would appear. He reached into his coat pocket for his torch but there was so much light from the moon that it seemed pointless to turn it on.

As the voices came closer St Clair saw that they belonged to two young women. They were as pretty as money and St Clair was heartened by the presence of such beauty to enliven his night patrol. He greeted them with his unique brand of sweet talk, 'Goodnight fair ladies. Will you allow a lonely policeman to join your delightful company and see you home?'

The young women laughed merrily at his manner of speech and one of them said, 'You don't even know where we live, yet you so eager to see us home!'

'Ah, but your home can't be very far away or such

lovely young ladies would not be out so late?' rejoined St Clair.

'You are right Mr St Clair,' said the other lady. 'We live just a little way from here and we welcome your protection. Who knows what we might meet on the way.'

St Clair was quite taken aback when he heard her call his name for he did not recognise either of the women, and he had not mentioned his name. But he supposed that he was well-known in the district. Besides he could not see their faces clearly and could not be sure that he had not spoken to one of them on some previous occasion. So he let it pass.

'Tell me,' he asked them. 'How far away do you live?'

'Just over a mile,' replied the one who had called him by name.

As they walked along St Clair wondered if his eyes were deceiving him. No matter how quickly he walked he could not catch up with those ladies and yet they did not appear to be walking fast. He began to feel uneasy. He noticed little things which he had missed when he first began to escort them. He could not hear the sound of their shoes on the road. In fact he could not tell whether they wore shoes for their feet were hidden by long dresses. He was about to get his torch out when one of them said to him, 'We are nearly home, Mr St Clair. Will you take our hands and help us down?'

St Clair looked and saw that she was pointing in the direction of The Intake. She held out her hand to take his but instead of taking her arm, he took out his torch and shone the beam of light right on her.

He only managed to catch a glimpse of her face

43

before the two women screamed and fled away from the piercing light of the torch. In a moment they were swallowed up in the forest of trees which were so close together that not even the moon's bright light could penetrate the darkness. Terror-stricken, St Clair fled down the mountain to the safety and bright lights of the main road.

When St Clair reported the incident to his Superintendent he said, 'Nonsense St Clair. A big man like you allow yourself to be fooled by two young ladies

out to tease you! Man, you should be ashamed of yourself.'

But St Clair says he knows what he knows and the Super can say what he likes; no one is getting St Clair to patrol that road again. For when he looked into the face of the lady nearest him he saw two empty sockets where there should have been eyes!

4. L'Esprits

People say that L'esprits, or the spirits we sometimes see, are the souls of those who died without finding peace. In different parts of the Caribbean they may be called jumbies, jack o'lanterns, ghosts, or duppies.

At certain times and seasons, spirits have greater freedom to move about and to show themselves to human beings in unusual encounters . . .

It was Hallowe'en, or the festival of the dead, and Young Desmond was hurrying to get home before midnight. He had to cross a small coconut grove and it was the last place he wanted to be on a night like Hallowe'en for it was said to be haunted by the ghosts of pirates and buccaneers buried there.

He was nearly half-way through the grove when he heard a rustling sound behind him but he told himself that it was only the wind rustling dried leaves on the ground. But as he walked on he realised that there were footsteps, firm footsteps behind him. And yet, how could that be? There had been no sound when he set out.

Desmond lengthened his stride without actually running. He did not have to strain his ears to hear that the footsteps were still there. They were getting closer even, though his companion did not seem to be walking any faster. The pace was the same as when he first heard it. As the distance between Desmond and his companion lessened he heard another sound. It was the rattle of wood knocking on wood. Or could it be bone on bone? Desmond broke out in a cold sweat.

Suddenly the footsteps were alongside and keeping pace with Desmond's footsteps. Desmond was too terrified to turn his head to see who walked beside him. He heard a rhythmical clicking sound with every tread. The walker matched him step for step. The echo of a voice without body and without colour ricocheted on the still night air until the grove was filled with

49

many sounds: 'Young maaaaaannnnn, whyyyyyyyyy arrrr youuuuuinnnsuchhhh a hurryyyyy?'

Desmond fought to control the panic that gripped him like a pair of giant pincers. It seemed an eternity before he could draw enough breath to speak and then his words came by fits and starts. 'I'm trying ... to to to ... get ... get hoome ... before ... midni .ni .. night but I ... have ... not ... not heard the ... church clock chime. Can you ttt ... tell me the time?'

'Certainly,' replied his companion. 'It was gone midnight when I left Hell!'

To this day Desmond does not remember how he got home and he still shivers with fear at the thought of his encounter with the spirit in the grove. And nothing will ever make him leave his house again on Hallowe'en night.

Frederic's Crossing

In the days when few people owned cars and only the city roads were lit by electricity, not many people risked wandering too far from home at night.

But love gives courage to the fainthearted and Frederic was in love with a girl in a distant village. Three times a week he mounted his horse and journeyed afar to court his fiancée. He had to cross a river to get there, and on the opposite bank of that river grew a silk cotton tree which was said to be the home of spirits.

Though Frederic wasn't a man to be daunted by superstitious belief, neither was he prepared to court danger. So he found a shallow part of the river a few miles downstream from the silk cotton tree and placed some large stones to provide his horse with a firm footing across the river. To this day the place is called 'Frederic's Crossing'.

On Hallowe'en night, which is also called All Souls' Night, Frederic was getting ready to visit his fiancée when his mother said to him, 'Frederic, you know that this is the night for spirits to roam and work their wicked schemes. Why don't you stay home, boy?'

But Frederic had promised his girl that he would visit that night and he intended to keep his promise. However, to calm his mother's fears he said, 'Ma, I promise that I will get home early tonight, long before the spirits start to roam.'

His mother was not satisfied with his reply. She felt that Frederic was making light of serious matters, so she said, 'With all the spirits of the dead and the un-dead, not to mention those human beings who like to turn spirit at night, how you know what time they will start roaming?'

Her protests fell on deaf ears. Frederic refused to change his plans. When she saw that he was deter-mined to go out, his mother took off her rosary beads and put them around his neck saying, 'Son, if I can't stop your foolishness, the least you can do is to wear these beads for protection.'

Frederic set out and nothing strange happened until he was returning home. First he ran into a terrible storm which turned the dirt road into a quagmire and slowed down his horse. Then the loud peals of thunder and the bright flashes of lightning made the animal so nervous that it bolted from the path and Frederic spent a great deal of time coaxing it back on to the right road. By the time Frederic reached the track which led to the river it was after midnight.

About half-a-mile from the river his horse refused to

go any further. Frederic pleaded with it, he kicked it, he whipped it but not an inch would it budge until a flash of lightning lit up the path. The horse was startled into action but in its panic it took the last road Frederic wanted to be on. The horse was heading for the silk cotton tree.

Long before Frederic saw the tree he heard a babel of unearthly sounds – a medley of groans, sighs and weeping. Frederic saw the tree as he came around a bend. It stood out clearly against the surrounding darkness, reflecting a sickly light. Long colourless hands snaked out of the branches, seeking, beckoning. As Frederic rode under the tree, his horse baulked for a moment and a pair of hands, all bones and cold as death, reached down and touched his head. Frederic knew without being told that those hands were trying to pierce his brain and seize his soul.

In that moment he felt the beads of the necklace his mother had placed around his neck and he began to pray as he had never prayed before. With one sprint the horse plunged into the river and as it did so, Frederic felt something hit his back and bounce off into the river with a loud plopping sound. The horse needed no further urging and soon horse and rider were on the other side of the river in the safety of their own village.

When Frederic's mother heard the story she wasted no time in asking the priest to come and perform a purifying ceremony over her son for she said, 'The spirits mark you with that eye that hit your back and that can only mean one thing. They want your soul and they will get it unless the priest cleans it off with holy water.' And this time there was no argument from Frederic.

The Locked Room

Ignatius Dolly was a self-made man who, according to
him, was given nothing by his parents but his name.
By the time he reached his fiftieth birthday he was
master of a thriving cocoa estate and employed more
than one hundred workers.

No one would deny that Dolly was a good provider
for his family but even they would agree that he was
a hard man.

'Nothing for nothing! That's my motto. I pay a fair
day's wage for an honest day's work and that's more
than most of my kind can say,' was Dolly's constant
boast. And anyone in trouble was foolish in appealing
to Dolly for help. He had neither sympathy nor money
to waste.

He built a comfortable house for his large family. As
his wealth grew, he added another building where he
carried out his business transactions. The building had
three rooms, used as offices. One was kept locked and
no one but Dolly allowed to enter it.

One day a new overseer came to work on the estate
and was immediately curious about the locked room.
He was a man who couldn't bear to leave a mystery
unsolved: and he was determined to find out what
Dolly kept there. He began to hang about the vicinity
of the building after work and one night he saw Dolly
enter the office. He pressed his ear against the wall but
the wall was so thick that the sounds within were muf-
fled. When Dolly failed to appear at midnight the
overseer gave up his watch and went to his quarters.

From that time the overseer doubled his efforts to
find a way of entering the locked office but every plan

failed. After a year it was clear that the only way into the room was through the door. There was only one key which would open it and that key was on a chain which Dolly wore around his neck awake and sleeping.

Then one night the overseer saw Dolly enter the room, and this time he did not lock the door behind him. The overseer's heart gave a leap, and after quickly looking around to see that no one else was in sight, he approached the door. It was slightly ajar and there was a peculiar light, not sharp and bright like the light given off by an electric bulb, but a warm golden glow.

The overseer pushed the door open and stepped into

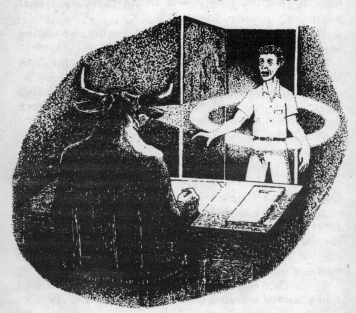

the room at the same time. The room was lit not by lamp, candle or electricity but by a figure seated behind a desk in one corner of the room – a figure with the body of a man and the head of a bull. From this head emanated a golden glow which made a pool of light in the dark room. As the overseer watched in amazement the head began to grow larger and larger and the circle of light widened in circumference until the overseer stood within it.

The blood pounded in his head and his eyes bulged with fear. Terror and fascination held him spellbound for what seemed to him an eternity. Finally he came to his senses and ran from the room. Carried by his instinct for survival, he ran from the estate and far far away from that dread apparition.

Hours later, Dolly came out of the room, a smug look on his face. As he locked the door he said to himself, 'Another spying busybody who'll never cross this threshold again.'

In the morning the police paid a visit to Dolly's estate to inform him that one of his workers had been found about three miles away lying dead on the side of the road. Cause of death had been diagnosed by the local doctor as a massive heart attack!

The Guitarist

Joe was always in demand for the Singings, or community evenings held in villages which were too far away from the city to enjoy its attractions. He was an excellent guitarist and when he wasn't performing on his own, he accompanied the singers and dancers who also attended the Singing.

After a Singing someone was sure to offer Joe a lift back to his village but on one occasion he found himself stranded miles away from his home with no choice but to set out on foot. It was a dark night and there wasn't a soul to be seen on the road, not even a cat or a dog, so Joe began to strum his guitar to hearten himself for the lonely journey ahead.

Joe had heard many stories about strange things seen at night on that road but he told himself that most of the people who related these stories had been drinking heavily. All the same, as he came to a cross-road known to be the haunt of Lajables and other restless spirits, he strummed his guitar loudly to drown the rising clamour of fearful thoughts in his head. In the quiet of early morning the tune was sharp and strong, and Joe began to move to the rhythm; but all the while his eyes were fixed on a point ahead of him where four roads met. The nearer he got, the more convinced he was that someone was standing in the middle of the road. He hoped with all his heart that he was wrong and that the shape was only a shadow cast by an overhanging tree.

The man stood so still he might have been a statue, and it was only when Joe was within arm's length of the figure that he saw any sign of life. The man was quite tall, and so thin that his clothes hung on him as though they were thrown over a wire frame. There was a musty smell about them. It was too dark to see who the man was or what he looked like, and when he spoke his voice had a rasp to it which set Joe's teeth on edge.

'You play a real fine guitar for a youngster,' said the man, falling into step beside Joe.

Just a little while before, Joe would have given anything to meet another human being but somehow he was not keen to have this man as a companion. Nevertheless his motto was 'Better to be safe than sorry' so he was as polite as his unease would allow.

'It's nothing special but I like to keep my hand in. What about you, man? Can you play guitar too?' asked Joe.

'Let me try your guitar and we'll see if I can match you,' replied the man. Joe handed over his guitar and the man began to play so gently and softly that Joe had to listen closely to hear the tune. He had never heard such a mournful air. But soon the music changed, the tune became wild and the rhythm fast and there was a harshness about it which drew a response from every nerve in Joe's body. Suddenly there was a new tone and mood and the music became light and enchanting. Joe felt as if he were borne in the air like a blown-up balloon. He was floating on a current of music and would follow it to the ends of the earth and beyond.

And then the music stopped. Joe came down to earth with a shock as he realized that he was standing in front of his house. The night clouds were slowly dispersing. The man handed the guitar back to Joe who was still dazed.

'Man, that was guitar music like I never heard in this world before,' said Joe.

'True?' said the man. 'You should have heard me when I was alive!'

The Devil's Mare

Two policemen, Milt and Cassie, were patrolling their beat late one night. As they approached a railway crossing Cassie said to Milt, 'Look over there, Milt. Tell me what you see?'

Milt's eyes followed the line of Cassie's pointing arm and peered into the darkness beyond it. 'I can't see anything outa place, Cassie. It's just one pool of blackness to me,' replied Milt.

'Don't give me that, man,' said Cassie heatedly. 'I can see a white horse as plain as I can see you. What's more, I'm taking it down to the station.' And he went to catch the horse.

No sooner had Cassie touched the bridle than the animal took off. It galloped away with the speed of a race horse, dragging Cassie along, clinging to the reins. Milt heard the horse's hooves but all he could see was Cassie, hands clasped moving through space.

Milt was standing in the same place when the Lance-Corporal came by on his nightly check. Dazed by what he had witnessed Milt tried to describe the incident but his story became more and more confused.

'What cock-and-bull story you telling me? Look here, Constable, you find that good-for-nothing Cassie wherever he is taking a nap before I pass back on my rounds. If he ain't here alongside you I shall be making a report about the two of you to the Super,' the Lance-Corporal warned.

He turned to walk back to his car.

There was nothing and no one in sight on that long straight main road. Suddenly out of nowhere, a cyclist came riding at the speed of a high wind. His bicycle was the normal size and so was he; yet he rode straight through the legs of the Lance-Corporal, flinging him high in the air and causing him to break his wrist as he fell.

By the time the two men came to their senses the cyclist had disappeared. Milt had to help the Lance-Corporal back to the station. Then he set out to look for Cassie but it was not until dawn that he found him, lying in the middle of the savannah on the outskirts of the town. Cassie was fast asleep and had suffered nothing worse than a few bruises.

Milt and Cassie searched high and low throughout the town for a white horse. They never found one but an old woman said that she remembered a story her mother had told her about a white horse. It went like this:

A certain man in the district made a pact with the devil, who promised to give him a horse that would never lose a race. In return the man would have to give up a soul when the devil asked for it. The foolish man agreed in the belief that he could offer one of his workmen as the victim but when the devil came for payment he asked for the man's daughter. The man begged the devil to spare the girl. She was all that he had, his wife having died in childbirth, but the devil would not budge. So the man put two bullets in his gun – one silver and one steel.

He went down to the stables where the horse – a mare – was kept and he fired the silver bullet into the back of its neck killing it instantly. Then he pointed the gun at his own heart and fired.

The old woman said that since that time many people have seen a white horse galloping around the savannah and sometimes, around the town, but no one has ever been able to catch it because it is the spirit of the devil's mare.

When Milt and Cassie told the Lance-Corporal the story he said to them, 'Just take your mind off spirit horses and start looking for the cyclist that knocked me down. I have a broken wrist to prove that *he* is no spirit.'

Yet to Milt and Cassie that is the strangest part of the night's events because it's hard to understand how a man on a bicycle could ride through somebody's legs!

It wasn't long after the incident of the mysterious white horse and the cyclist that Milt and Cassie were again on night patrol in the same town. On this occasion, they had just finished a circuit of the area to the north of the town centre. The terrain was hilly and steep and the roads, little more than gravel tracks, were hard on the feet.

On the side of the road in front of the Community Hall was a wooden bench, its legs firmly bedded down in the ground. Here Cassie halted and with a groan of relief stretched himself out on the seat. 'Milt, boy,' he said. 'I must take five before we go on down this hill.'

'And suppose the Super come and find you laid out as though you're on your sleep-easy at home. What then?' asked Milt.

'To hear you talk a body would think I said five hours not five minutes,' retorted Cassie. 'Okay, Milt, you go down and if the Super come, it's my funeral.'

Milt had gone some distance when it occurred to him that he had not heard footsteps. He was sure that

60

he had been walking for at least ten minutes. He was angry with Cassie. He felt that he was always looking out for him and covering up for him and that Cassie never thanked him for all that he did.

'Since he so determined to tangle with the Super let him stew in his own juice,' fumed Milt and he continued on his way without so much as a backward glance. Somehow behind the anger there was a murmur of doubt. Milt was nearly half-way down the hill; Cassie should have started out long before this. Suddenly Milt made up his mind to swallow his pride, and turned around. As he climbed the hill he could hear no sound of anyone coming down. The doubts rose from murmur to clamour. 'What the blazes is the matter with Cassie?' he exploded but the sound of his voice did nothing to lessen the fear he felt. He was convinced that something terrible had happened to his friend. He began to run as fast as he could up the steep hill.

Panting heavily he came at last to the place where he had left Cassie and he saw him, still lying on the bench.

Cassie called out, 'Milt, give me hand up. I can't raise meself.'

'Cassie, stop this foolishness and get up, man,' replied Milt. He could see no reason why Cassie could not get up on his own accord.

'I'm serious, Milt. I've been trying to get up since you left me. Help me up,' pleaded Cassie.

Milt heard the fear in Cassie's voice and he saw how hard he was straining to move himself. He stretched out his hands and took hold of Cassie's and pulled hard. It was useless. It felt as though Cassie was glued to the bench.

61

'I feel as though a heavy weight is pressing me down, Milt,' said Cassie.

Milt was worried. He had never seen Cassie in such a state. He was torn between the urge to go and get help, and the fear of leaving Cassie on his own. While he was making up his mind, he heard Cassie breathe deeply and shift himself.

'Cassie boy, you all right?' he enquired anxiously.

'Quick, Milt, give me a hand. I think I can get up now,' said Cassie.

Milt supported Cassie under his arms and helped him into a sitting position and after a short while, Cassie was able to set off with Milt down the hill.

Months later Milt and Cassie were attending a Nine Nights ceremony to commemorate a death. It was held in a house not far from the place where Cassie had rested on the bench. As the evening wore on generous helpings of rum loosened the tongues of those present and a flood of stories was released.

After Cassie had told the story of his brief paralysis on the bench an old man said, 'Sir, I will tell you a story and perhaps you will understand what happened that night.'

'A story! What story?' exclaimed Cassie.

'When I was a boy,' began the old man. 'It had a mayor in this town called Dumas and a more selfish and mean-spirited man I have never met. So when he presented a bench to the town, everyone was surprised. But not for long for it turned out that he only did it to impress the Governor who was due to visit the town. He had his name engraved on the bench and placed it right in front of the Community Hall where the Governor could see it.

'But when the Governor arrived he hardly looked at the bench even though Dumas kept stopping in front of it. And when the Governor made his speech he never mentioned the bench, or the mayor for that matter. People say he did it to spite Dumas for putting his name on the bench.

'Dumas was hopping-mad and as soon as the Governor left he announced that no one was to sit on the bench but himself. Every day, at lunch time he would leave the Town Hall, and sit on the bench and if he should spot anybody sitting on it, well, crapaud smoke you pipe, Dumas would make sure that you suffered in some way.

'One day Dumas sat on the bench much longer than usual. A passer-by noticed this and spoke to him. When Dumas didn't answer, the man looked closely at his face. Dumas was stone-cold dead and as stiff as a ramrod.

'After Dumas died a few people sat on the bench but they never did it more than once. Each one of them said that they felt a heavy cold weight on them when they tried to get up. And try as they might they could not move until that weight lifted.'

'Surely you don't believe that a dead man could be responsible for whatever happened to those people and to Cassie?' asked Milt.

'All I know,' said the old man, 'is that Dumas swore after the Governor left, that no one would ever enjoy *his* bench but himself. And no one ever has.'

63

5. Le Diable

Le Diable (Djab) or devil is the master of all supernatural beings. He can take any form he wishes. In stories from the Caribbean he usually appears as a natty dresser and a well-spoken man. He strikes bargains with human beings, offering gold, wealth, success in exchange for their services and their souls. He is supposed to be powerful and clever yet there are many stories about mere human beings outsmarting him ...

A man who had lost his way in a very remote part of the countryside was invited by a woman to spend the night in her house. He was in the middle of a most enjoyable evening meal – pounded breadfruit and saltfish buljol, a fricasee with sliced onions – when he heard something hit the roof – bodoop!

He looked at the woman, expecting her to say something about it, but she continued eating as though nothing had happened. A few minutes later he heard the same sound – bodoop! It was quickly followed by two sounds, one after the other – bodoop! bidiff!

The man could contain his curiosity no longer so he said to the woman, 'Madam, your breadfruit must be over-ripe that so many are falling tonight.'

'Breadfruit!' replied the woman. 'Man, that ain't breadfruit. What you hear is my neighbour John signalling.'

The man could make neither head nor tail of this explanation and asked, 'But what is so urgent at this time of night that John has to signal?'

'Well,' replied the woman. 'He throwing skulls to remind me that we should be on our way to visit the devil. When he don't see me leave the house he will go and bring the devil to see me.'

'Bon Dieu sans yeux!' exclaimed the man leaping up from the table and without waiting to gather up his belongings he ran helter-skelter from the house. Once outside he did not stop to check whether he was travelling east, west, north or south but took the road

67

straight ahead and did not slacken his speed until he was clear of that village.

Bravé dangé

High up in the mountains there is a tiny village. As dusk falls the people lock the doors of their houses and fill the holes and cracks in the walls with newspaper to keep out the spirits. Candles and gas lamps are lit and shed their glow in dark corners but outside it is pitch black and the night is full of strange noises.

In this village there was a young man called Patrick who did not believe in spirits any more than he believed that there was a man in the moon. Over and over his mother warned him about the many dangers of the night saying, 'With my own eyes I have seen Lajables who appears as a beautiful girl. She can fool you with her soft words and pretty ways and lead you right into danger unless you know what to do.'

Patrick said, 'But Mama, shall I hide indoors because of a girl with a bad foot when I have two good legs?'

'And what about the soucouyant that flies at night sucking blood like a vampire? Tell me, what will you do to that one?' asked his mother.

'I will catch it and wrap my coat around it and put it out like the flame of a candle,' teased Patrick.

His mother was so angry that he was making light of her beliefs that she didn't bother to ask him what he would do about the djab-djab with their painted bodies, their twitching tails and eyes red as a harvest moon. If she had, Patrick would have treated the devils as casually as he did the other supernatural beings.

68

But nothing is secret in a small village. News travels fast and the word soon got around that Patrick was acting like a bravé dangé. When the other young men heard about it they forgot their private squabbles and joined forces to shame Patrick.

'So he think he is a fearless man!' said one of the youths. 'Well, when we finish with him everybody will find out whether he is a bravé dangé for truth.'

One night nine of them disguised themselves. They wrapped white sheets around their bodies, painted their faces like devils and hid in the canefield near Patrick's house. He had gone to a Carnival dance at the Village Hall and was about to enter when a drunken man staggered out of the Hall and fell down on the side of the road. There he lay quite unconscious. The man wore the costume of a devil and a devil's mask. Patrick thought to himself, 'What a waste of a good costume. I shall borrow it just for tonight and return it tomorrow when he is sober.' So he put on the costume and mask and went into the Hall where he won a prize for his disguise. When the dance was over he set off home in high spirits and well-pleased with his good fortune.

The church clock was chiming twelve midnight as Patrick walked along the dirt road that led to his house. The youths hiding in the canefield could not see who was coming but they heard footsteps which sounded like Patrick's. At a given signal they leaped out on to the path in front of him shouting, 'C'est nous neuf diables!' We are nine devils! 'C'est nous neuf diables!'

Imagine their surprise when they saw before them what appeared to be the devil himself. A pair of coal-black eyes gleamed from a face as white as chalk from

69

which two large pointed ears stuck out. A blood-red mouth grinned wickedly at them. This devil shouted more loudly and leaped higher than any of the youths and as he pranced amongst them his long tail looped and coiled like an angry snake.

Frightened out of their wits the youths ran through the dark streets clutching their sheets and calling on the village saints to save them. A pack of dogs, determined on getting their piece of flesh for being disturbed from slumber, pursued the boys. The few which did not give chase made up for it by adding their protests to the shrieks and prayers of the youths. Never had there been such pandemonium in the village as on that night. Every one was roused from sleep although not one of them dared look out to see what was happening.

But the villagers still talk about that night when they heard the fiendish laughter of the devil and the screams of his horde of demons. 'Oui,' they insist, 'le diable lui-même.' The devil himself. For did they not hear with their own ears the devil's voice above all others, shouting, 'C'est nous dix diables!' We are ten devils. 'C'est nous dix diables!'

Never Play with Fire

A young man was walking along a road one night bemoaning his bad fortune.

'O life!' he cried. 'So this is what you bring me to. You rob me of house and home, you rob me of friends and I don't even have a place to lay my head. O life! I would give my soul for a crust of bread.'

Just then he saw a figure coming towards him. As

it drew near, the young man made out a very tall man with eyes that seemed to smoulder in the dark. He was elegantly dressed in a frilled white shirt and a well-tailored suit. When he spoke his voice was as smooth as butter.

'I could not help but overhear your words. Truly life has not been kind to you. Even so you must be in a bad state to make so rash an offer,' the tall man said.

'Sir, nothing could be worse than what I suffer these last three years. Not even the loss of a soul.' replied the young man.

Still the stranger pressed, 'Do you mean that you would exchange a soul for bread and bed?'

His taunting manner annoyed the young man. 'Look at me, man! Look at the condition of my bare feet! Look at the rags I wear! That is what people judge me by when I ask for a job, a piece of bread, or a bed for the night. Yes, I can do without a soul.'

'Good,' said the stranger. 'Since you are so sure, I will make a bargain with you. I will give you the opportunity to become successful but one day I shall return for the payment of a soul. Is it a deal?'

Well, anyone with a grain of sense would have backed down, said some 'Hail Marys,' or taken to his heels but the young man was desperate and decided to brazen it out. He agreed. The following morning he came to his senses but it was too late. The contract was sealed and stamped. The stranger had vanished.

Time passed and the young man forgot all about the incident. He found a job as an assistant manager on a large cocoa estate and a year later, when the manager died in a mysterious way, he was promoted. And a good manager he was too for the estate flour-

71

ished. The family who owned the estate became more and more dependent on the young man's advice and their generosity knew no bounds. Only one thing was lacking to make his happiness complete.

His employers had an only child, a beautiful and modest daughter. The young man had fallen deeply in love with her and he knew she was fond of him. Yet he held back from telling her how he felt.

One day the girl's father took him aside and said, 'My boy, have you ever thought of getting married?'

The question was so sudden that the young man was at a loss for words. He had to play for time until he knew which way the wind was blowing.

'Sir,' he replied. 'You know that marriage got teeth and need much thought and time. All my thoughts are on the estate and I have no time to think about a wife.'

The father was pleased with the young man's reply. True, he had not heard the young man's name linked with any of the local girls but he had to make sure.

'Well then,' said the father. 'Let me make you a proposition. Would you consider marriage with my daughter? I believe she is fond of you and the estate will be in good hands when I am dead and gone.'

The young man was beside himself with joy and lost no time in proposing to the girl. She accepted the offer of marriage willingly and soon preparations for the wedding were in full swing. The young man spent most of his spare time designing and building fittings and furniture for the new house which the girl's parents had given them as a wedding present. He was an excellent craftsman and put his heart and soul into making things which were beautiful as well as useful. But now his luck took a bad turn.

73

One evening he was working late on a piece of furniture when suddenly he felt so cold that his hands were seized with cramp and he could not hold the tools. He shivered and as he went to close the open door he saw a man framed in the doorway.

'I see that you are doing well, very well indeed,' said a voice which stirred a memory. 'Now it is time for payment and the keeping of a promise.'

'Who are you?' enquired the young man peering at the stranger's face which was hidden in shadow.

'I met you five years ago poor, hungry and in rags and offered you all that you have now,' said the visitor coming into the room so that the young man could see his face.

There was no need to do so for the young man had suddenly remembered that hypnotic voice which had tempted him to make a rash deal, a deal which might now cost him more than life. Every limb of his body trembled at the thought of it, but the same fear that made him shake as if in a fever, sharpened his wits.

'You are a fair-minded man,' he said. 'So let me first set everything in order with my employer and I will pay you what I owe.'

'Very well,' said the man. 'I will give you seven days and then I shall return to hold you to your bargain.'

The young man could not sleep that night for thinking how he might save his soul. And he was tortured with visions of indescribable horror. He moaned and tossed and wept, 'Ay-a-ay! To have come so near to Paradise only to be dragged deep into Hell.'

Early next morning he set out to see an old Spanish woman who lived at the top of the mountain. He told her about his meeting with the tall man who had

74

promised him all he desired and had now returned to take his soul.

'Man, when you play with fire you must expect to get burn,' she said. 'It is El Diablo himself you gambling your life with and maybe I can help or maybe I cannot. I will do what I can.'

She gave him a special prayer to repeat seven times a day for seven days of waiting. She gave him a crucifix to wear around his neck. Last of all she gave him something wrapped in a black cloth which she placed in a small wooden box. 'You must see no one for the seven days and no food must pass your lips but water. When the devil comes, give him the box. He alone must open it and until he does you will not know what is inside.'

When the young man left the old woman he went directly to his employer and asked for one week's leave to attend to important business. Then he returned home, locked his door and began his vigil. On the seventh day he awoke early and placed the box on the table near him. The day passed slowly and night came. Not a cricket chirped and the nightly chorus of frogs was hushed.

A few minutes after midnight there was a strong gust of wind which broke the door off its hinges and sent it crashing to the floor. At the same time the lights flickered and went out leaving the place in darkness. The young man did not move from his seat near the table, but his hands tightened around the box which the old woman had given him. He waited.

The room was lit up by a figure outlined by a circle of flames. The strong stench of sulphur filled the young man's nostrils; his attention was held by a pair of eyes which burned into his head destroying his will. Silently he began to recite the prayer that the old woman had given him and soon there was no fire in his head. A voice spoke, 'I have come to complete our bargain.' The young man handed him the box without a word.

'Why do you give me this?' asked the voice. The young man remained silent.

The stranger opened the box and unwrapped the cloth. His sharp intake of breath sounded like the hiss of a viper before it strikes its victim.

'How dare you mock me?' he asked and the venom in his soft voice sent a chill through the young man, who in turn looked at the contents of the box. All hope left him. He had been so sure that the old woman had given him some holy relic which would terrify the evil one and send him scuttling back to hell. Instead she had placed the SOLE of a shoe in a box!

The words went round and round in his brain 'THE SOLE OF A SHOE! THE SOLE OF A SHOE FOR HIS SOUL!' Then he heard himself speaking words which seemed to come from outside him, 'It is true that we made a deal,' he said. 'But you never spelt out exactly what you wanted of me and you will agree that the word has many meanings. Why, it might be the underside of my foot, or again, it might be a fish. And surely it could also be part of a plough, or even ...' He never finished the list of what the word might have meant. The devil (for he it was) threw down the box and its contents on the floor and disappeared into a bright yellow flame which floated through the door, and was gone.

The young man breathed deeply for the first time in seven days. Then he wept a little from sheer relief, and who could blame him? He had gone through a terrible ordeal – one which he would never forget as long as he lived. As for the sole of the shoe, he wrapped it in the black cloth and stored it safely in the box to remind him of his narrow escape. And if you look at the sole carefully you can still see the scorch marks where the devil held it.

6. Douennes

There is a popular belief that children who die before they are baptised become lost souls and are doomed to wander the earth. The Douennes, which haunt the forest and are sometimes seen playing near rivers, are said to be spirits of such children.

From a distance a Douenne could be mistaken for a real child. A closer look would reveal that the 'child' had no eyes, no ears and no mouth or nose. Its hair might be either thick and matted, or worn in two long pigtails. But the strangest feature of the Douenne is its feet, which are always turned backwards.

These elvish creatures trick children into following them by imitating the calls of hide-and-seek ...

Lost Children of the Forest

In a seaside village a little girl used to take a short cut through the wood which separated her school from home. She enjoyed playing in the river which wound its way in and out of the wood and then flowed down to the sea.

One afternoon, on her way home, she heard cries of 'Whoop! Whoop!' coming from inside the wood. The little girl set off in the direction of the voices which sounded like other children at play. In a clearing she saw three children who were dressed somewhat oddly in loose white shifts. They wore straw hats with wide brims which covered most of their faces.

As soon as they saw the little girl they ran off, still shouting their cries of 'Whoop! Whoop!'. The child hesitated. She wasn't sure that she wanted to play with these children after all. Suddenly she saw one of them peeping at her from behind a tree. The strange child held out a bright-red pomerac and the little girl, who loved the sweet juicy pomerac more than any other fruit, began to walk towards the tree.

When she got to the tree there was no one. She saw footprints but they were all pointing towards her. The little girl began to feel afraid for she found herself in a part of the wood where she had not been before. But the scent of the fruit was strong and the little girl was tempted to go on.

'Whoop! Whoop!' she heard the voices again and they sounded close.

She glimpsed a white shift for a moment and then it was gone. She began to walk faster and faster to catch up with the children. The footprints became difficult to see for the sun was sinking fast and the trees cast shadows. The little girl could no longer hear the cries. She began to run backwards and forwards, looking in vain for the path which led to the road. Finally she sat down and began to sob loudly.

A stone's throw away, a hunter heard the child. At first he thought it might be Douennes up to their mischievous pranks especially as his dog started to howl and tried to run off. Tightening his grip on the animal's collar the hunter walked towards the sound of the crying.

As he led the little girl out of the wood the hunter heard what sounded like the yelping of a wild beast. Immediately his dog began to whimper and the hairs on its back stood as straight and sharp as pine needles. The hunter didn't dare slacken his hold on the dog for he knew without a doubt that the Douennes were trying to lure it away from him by imitating the sounds of an animal. If they could not destroy the child then they would do their utmost to harm the dog.

The journey out of the wood was a nightmare for the hunter. On the one hand the child was so terrified that she had to be coaxed, one step at a time, and she clung to the hunter so tightly that he could hardly move himself. Then there was the dog, pulling and tugging every inch of the way to escape from the evil sounds and scents of the Douennes.

At last the hunter reached the safety of the village and took the little girl home. And although she soon got over her fright, the hunter's dog was never the same again and could never be persuaded to set foot (or paws) in any wood or forest after that day.

The Sound of Crying

A woman was on her way home one night when she saw a black kitten sitting in the middle of a crossroad. The kitten was mewing so plaintively that the woman picked it up and took it home. She warmed some milk and set it down in a saucer. After the kitten drank its fill, the woman placed it in a basket in the kitchen, closed the door and went to bed.

In the middle of the night she was awakened by the cry of a baby. She turned on the light and looked around her room. She looked in her sitting-room and in her bathroom but saw no one so she went back to bed. Not long afterwards she was roused from sleep once more by the sound of crying. There was no doubt about it. Someone was crying, and that someone was inside her house. But how could that be? Suddenly it occurred to her that it might be the kitten which she had brought home that night. She went straightaway to the kitchen and opened the door.

The woman could hardly believe what she saw for standing at the kitchen window was the figure of a small child. It was whimpering, but, strangely, there was not an ounce of feeling in the sounds. The woman went towards the child; suddenly the light from the moon lit up the kitchen and she saw that it was faceless. Quickly she looked at its feet.

'O mi Lord,' she cried. 'This is a Douenne, dear Lord what's to be done with it?'

'What's to be done? What's to be done?' mocked the Douenne imitating the woman's voice.

Before the woman could recover from the surprise of hearing her words repeated in exactly her tone of voice, she heard a confusion of noises outside the house. Looking through the shutters she saw a host of small creatures. They were echoing the cries made by their spirit-kind inside the house, and they were beating on the doors trying to get in.

There was only one thing for it. The woman had to get the creature out at once. She tried to lift it but it was heavy as a pound of sin. Twice she tried and failed but the third time she remembered some prayers for souls in torment and recited them out loud. The Douenne became as light as a feather. The woman thrust it out quickly, made the sign of the cross and locked her door. Immediately the host of creatures disappeared and all was quiet again.

Since then nothing will persuade that woman to have a cat anywhere near the house and she keeps a large dog, who is the enemy of every cat in the neighbourhood.

7. Papa Bois

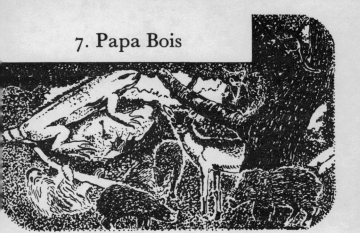

Papa Bois or Maître Bois as he is sometimes called, is the father of the forest and protector of wild life. People who live near forests, hunters and woodsmen have many stories to tell about this legendary figure . . .

A hunter had been tracking lappe, a wild animal which is much sought after because of its delicious taste. He had been hunting it for two days and each time he thought he had trapped it, it gave him the slip.

About noon on the third day he met an elderly man with thick, greying hair, a long unkempt beard and piercing black eyes. His body was as hairy as an animal's and his only garment was a pair of faded khaki shorts. A horn made of bamboo was attached to his waistband.

'Bonjour compère! How goes the hunting today?' enquired the old man.

'Bonjour!' replied the hunter. 'Not so good, old man. I sight a lappe two days ago and no matter how I try I can't corner that animal.'

'Let it be, man. Hunt something else. You will never catch lappe this season,' said the old man.

'O ho! like you know something that the rest of us don't know?' sneered the hunter.

'Reckon I do,' rejoined the old man. 'But tell me, do you think that you can match the instinct of that animal?'

'Speak plain, old man. I have no time for riddles,' said the hunter who was getting angry.

'And I, young man, have all the time in the world,' retorted the old man. And he turned on his heel and walked away before the hunter could think of a reply.

The hunter shrugged his shoulders and dismissed the old man's comments. He decided that the old man probably lived in the forest and had lost his reasoning powers from living alone for too long. He continued to track the lappe, and he followed its trail into the depths of the forest. He came to a place where the trees were so tall that you could not see their crowns, where the trees grew so close together that their trunks formed a gigantic corral. The hunter walked along this wall of trees and suddenly came upon an opening about the width of two men standing abreast.

He entered and found himself in another world – a world so silent that he could hear his heartbeats. The atmosphere was cool and fresh and not a breath of wind disturbed the stillness within the cavern of trees. There was just enough light to cast shadows and the hunter thought he saw the figure of someone in the shadows.

'Hello, is anyone here?' he called.

'Yes, I am here,' came a reply from someone quite near to him and he recognised the voice as that of the old man he had met earlier that day.

'I see you did not take my advice to leave the lappe alone,' said the old man. 'But since you are determined come with me.'

The old man led the way to a darkened cavern full of animals. The hunter could just make out the forms of manicou, agouti, wild pigs, and wild cats, deer, and birds of all kinds, as well as dozens of lappe. Some of the lappe were wounded and others were heavy with young.

'You wanted that lappe. Okay, go ahead and find it,' said the old man.

The hunter had long regretted his rash action in entering the strange cavern. He now realised that the old man was none other than Papa Bois and that he would have to use all his wits to escape the grave danger he faced. In the poor light it was difficult to identify the lappe which he had only seen at a distance. Then he remembered that more than once he had caught the scent of hog plums on the trail. He remembered too that hog plums were in season and that he had indeed, passed plum trees with several of the fruit on the ground. He reasoned that if the lappe had passed that way it might have eaten some of the plums.

Again and again he went the rounds of animals stopping frequently to sniff out the odours that came from them. He was on the point of giving up when he caught a whiff which was undoubtedly the smell of hog plum. He stopped and looked carefully at some animals in a corner. An animal was cowering far back in the group and when he picked it up it was wet with perspiration. He turned to Papa Bois and said, 'This is the lappe I was hunting but I no longer wish to harm her for I see that she is about to give birth.' And he set the animal loose again.

'Ah, now, Compère Hunter, perhaps you begin to understand our conversation this morning. But you must be tired after your long hunt. Come and rest a little while I bring you some refreshment,' said Papa Bois.

The hunter followed the old man who led him to a lighter part of the cavern. In it was a table made from the mahogany tree and on the table was a woven basket filled with fresh and sweet-smelling fruit. Around the table were seats of cane and bamboo, and seats which were shaped in coils and seemed to be made of animal skin. The old man motioned to the hunter to sit on one of the coiled seats and he was about to do so when he thought he saw a swift flick of red at the base of the seat. Carefully he felt one of the coils and found it warm to the touch. He moved away quickly and said, 'If you don't mind, Papa Bois I would rather have a cane seat.'

Papa Bois had been watching the hunter closely and saw that he had not been fooled by the snakes coiled to look like stools. 'Good, good, Compère Hunter. You learn fast and I see that with a little guidance you should make an excellent woodsman. But now you deserve a fine dinner and a good night's rest.' In no time Papa Bois had cooked and served up a rich vegetable soup and prepared a bed of fresh rushes from the river for the hunter to sleep on.

But the hunter did not go to sleep at once. In the stories told about Papa Bois there was one fact that was often repeated – as long as the old man gave his word he could be trusted but until then a person had to be on his guard at all times. He had heard terrible tales about people who had crossed the old man and ended up bewitched into wild animals themselves. The hunter noticed how often Papa Bois stroked his beautiful bamboo horn and he noted where he rested it that night.

The following morning when Papa Bois awoke and looked for his horn, it was not to be found. He went to the room where the hunter was sleeping and shook him awake.

'Is this how you repay me for my hospitality?' he asked the hunter. 'Where have you hidden my horn?'

'Papa Bois, your horn is of no use to me,' said the hunter, 'but I know that you value it highly and you may have it back as soon as you promise me my freedom.'

'I will not be threatened and I *will* find my horn,' said Papa Bois.

'Look, Papa Bois, I have learnt my lesson and I assure you that I shall not cross your path again. Why don't you agree to my freedom. You'll never guess where the horn is hidden.'

Papa Bois would not give in and the hunter began to think that he would never see the world outside again. But two days later after Papa Bois had looked everywhere, well almost everywhere, he agreed to let the hunter go and gave his word on it. Then the hunter told him where the horn was hidden. In fact it wasn't hidden at all but there for all the world to see. The hunter had unscrewed one of the bamboo joints on a seat and replaced it with the horn which, unless you looked hard, appeared to be just another bamboo joint of a stool.

Of course the hunter kept his word. He hunts no more in the forest but he collects snake skins and runs a thriving business making coiled snake-skin seats.

A Strange Hunting

One Friday three men from the city arrived in a small village and asked for someone to act as a hunting guide. They had heard that there was good game in the nearby forest.

The villagers hemmed and hawed and said that they had to speak to Joseph, the head of the village. When he arrived the men were so impressed by his confident manner that they agreed to hire him immediately. Joseph asked no payment except that the hunters leave for the villagers a third of whatever they shot.

Late that evening the hunting party set off. It was clear from the onset that Joseph was completely at home in the forest and the men following him did not doubt that their bags would be filled with game by morning. But they caught nothing that night or next day, and by evening, two of them were all for returning to the village. But the third man said, 'Look fellows, in for a penny, in for a pound. Let us wait one more night and who knows but that our luck might change.'

They kept watch through the night. Nothing stirred. Just before dawn the three men decided that they had had enough of waiting. When Joseph saw that they were determined to leave he said, 'I know that this forest is teeming with game. Wait a little longer and I will find some deer and send them in your direction.'

The hunters were not keen to spend any more time in the cold, dark forest but they agreed to wait for a few more hours. Before Joseph left he said to them, 'There's just one thing I must warn you about. When you see the herd there will be a big deer leading. Let him go. If you shoot him you will never hunt in this forest again.'

The hunters did not have long to wait. Suddenly a flock of birds took flight and soon after the men heard the sound of hooves. A large herd of deer came into sight and leading them was a huge stag with antlers, which were beautifully sculptured lines and curves. One of the hunters said, 'In a whole lifetime I'll never see a beast like that. Joseph can't be serious.' And pulling the trigger of his gun he shot the deer. It leapt in the air and uttered a scream that sounded human. Almost at once the entire herd disappeared. The hunters set off in pursuit and followed a trail of blood until

they came to a fortress of trees and vines. They
attacked it with cutlasses but no matter how they
slashed away they could not penetrate it.

One of them said, 'I don't know about you two but
I am getting out of this place. There's something funny
about the whole affair.'

The others agreed at once for they too were feeling
uneasy. They walked for a long time but it was not

until late afternoon that they found landmarks which led them out of the forest and back to the village.

It was nearly dusk when they arrived at the village square and a crowd of people were standing about. One old man came up to the men and asked, 'What did you do to Joseph?'

'You mean he came back here without us?' said one of the hunters. 'Where is he?'

'Yes, he came back,' replied the old man 'And no thanks to you either. He lost so much blood that it's a wonder he got as far as the village. We had to lift him and carry him to the doctor.'

'But how was he hurt?' persisted the hunter. 'We haven't seen him since early this morning.'

'Who shot him in his right shoulder then?' demanded the old man angrily. 'The three of you got guns and Joseph don't have a gun to his name.'

'Listen man, we didn't shoot anybody ...' began the hunter but even as he was saying the words a thought came into his head. His eyes widened with the shock of understanding.

'O my God,' he whispered. 'Not ...'

The old man nodded his head.

'Now you understand? Well, take my advice and leave before it is too late. The people in this village love Joseph and I wouldn't like to see the three of you hurt so go now.'

The men wasted no time in taking their leave. None of them has hunted in that or any other forest for fear of meeting Papa Bois whom they had wounded that day.

Merry Hildo

One day a hunter called Merry Hildo was hunting for wild hog in the forest when an old man greeted him: 'Young man give me your arm and walk me a little way.' Merry Hildo gave his arm to the old man and they set out together. But Merry Hildo was a cautious fellow and as he walked he reasoned to himself, 'Now what is such an old man doing so deep in the forest?' He looked at the old man and saw that he had neither gun, nor bag for game. But he saw a horn hanging from his belt.

'Good-oh!' thought Hildo. 'It's Papa Bois himself that is holding me tight, tight.' Hildo walked soft and he didn't say a word or give a look that would betray that he knew who his companion was. He just waited to see what Papa Bois would do.

After they had walked for about a mile and a half they came to a large wooden house. Papa Bois took out a giant-size key and opened the door. Inside the house was every kind of animal, bird and reptile but not one of them showed any fear or interest in Merry Hildo. Then Papa Bois led the hunter to a beautiful room in which were three of the prettiest girls Hildo had ever seen. These were Papa Bois' daughters.

'Sit down, young man,' said Papa Bois. 'It's not often that I have visitors and my daughters long for company.'

'I would consider it an honour to be their friend, that is, if you have no objection sir,' replied Hildo. At that moment he could think only of the beauty of the girls.

'All in good time,' said Papa Bois softly. 'We will

sup first and then talk about such matters. What is your favourite dish?'

Now there was nothing Hildo loved more than roasted wild hog but he wasn't fool enough to say so to Papa Bois. He replied, 'Well, I like a good fish stew.'

'Fine! Fine!' said Papa Bois. 'The girls will prepare something tasty for you in no time at all.'

And so it seemed to Hildo. He had barely settled himself in his chair before the girls came bustling in with steaming dishes which they placed on the table before him. There were dishes of fish cooked in ways which teased his nostrils and made his mouth water. He could hardly wait to be served.

At last Hildo's appetite was satisfied and the dishes were empty.

'And now,' said Papa Bois. 'Let us talk about you.'

'About me?' queried Hildo apprehensively. 'What about me?'

'No need to be so fearful,' said Papa Bois. 'Did you not offer friendship to my daughters a little while ago?'

'Oh yes, sir,' replied Hildo eagerly. He was relieved that it was no more than that.

'Well,' continued Papa Bois. 'How would you like to marry one of my daughters?'

Merry Hildo's mouth opened to utter an oath but he caught it in time. He was well aware of Papa Bois' cunning and he knew that there was more to this offer than met the eye. He pretended to be flattered.

'Papayo!' exclaimed Hildo. 'I never expected to have such good fortune. Give me some time to make up my mind.'

'Don't take too long, my friend. I'll give you half an hour,' said Papa Bois, and he left the room.

Merry Hildo was in a fine pickle. If he refused the offer his life was not worth a penny. Besides it made no difference which daughter was chosen, he would be an idiot to turn his back on a beautiful wife and a good cook into the bargain. He came to a decision.

'What is your choice?' enquired Papa Bois when he returned after the half hour was up.

'I will choose your youngest daughter for my bride,' said Hildo. He hoped that the youngest would also be the least experienced in the magic arts. Merry Hildo knew that his mortal soul was in danger and he would have to remain alert to survive the night. Papa Bois would use his daughter to bring about Hildo's downfall. But why?

That night the daughter he had chosen as wife practised every wile she knew on the hunter to lull him to sleep but he kept himself awake by silently reciting prayers. He must not relax for one moment. Eventually, the girl fell asleep and Hildo only closed his eyes when he heard her even breathing.

He rose at dawn and waited to see what would happen next. The two older sisters were standing outside his room when he opened the door in response to their knocking. It was clear from the look of surprise on their faces that it was not Hildo they had expected.

'Is everything well with our little sister?' they asked.

'Everything is well with your sister,' Hildo replied shortly and closed the door.

He looked at the girl who was now awake. She looked back at him with her large lovely dark eyes and he realised that he wanted her for his true wife, no matter what. He put his arms around her and spoke gently to her. 'Tell me truly if you want to be my wife and leave your father's house?' he asked.

99

'Yes,' she replied. 'Take me away with you and I will be a good wife to you.'

'If you are speaking the truth you will have to help me outsmart your father,' said Hildo.

The girl looked sideways and did not reply. But Hildo persisted.

'Why does your father wish to harm me? I have never offended him.'

'It is true that he will harm you if he can,' she admitted reluctantly. 'Some months ago you killed one of his favourite pets. It was a hog which he had taken from its mother as she lay dying in the forest. And my father nursed it as if it were his own child. He is still angry with you.'

'But how can he blame me for that? Hunting is my work and I have to work to live,' protested Hildo.

'Never mind,' said the girl. 'I will help you escape the punishment which my father has planned for you. Listen carefully to what I say:

'You must put on your shirt on the wrong side, and turn your hat inside out.

'You must take everything my father gives you with your left hand.

'You must leave the house walking backwards and close the door as you leave even though you close me inside the house.'

'But how do I know that he will allow you to come to me if I shut you in?' asked Merry Hildo.

'You must trust me,' replied the girl, 'and you must not look back until you have crossed the bridge over the stream yonder.'

Merry Hildo followed the girl's instructions to the letter. The hardest part was leaving her inside the house. When he was outside he took the path straight in front of him and followed it until he came to a mountain stream with such clear clean water that he could see the smallest stone at the bottom. He was tempted to look behind him but he remembered his promise to the girl. Even when he heard a loud splash in the stream he still did not look back until he was on the far side of the bridge. As he did so he saw the girl he had chosen as wife standing right behind him and she looked lovelier than ever.

'What was it that made the loud splash in the stream?' Hildo asked.

'My father knew that I had helped you so he inflicted on me the punishment he intended for you. When you left he changed me into a wild hog. But as long as you kept your promise until I crossed the stream, and was washed by the cleansing waters, I was safe. I knew that the water would change me back into human form. My father was also testing you to see if you are a man who can be relied on. We shall now both be forgiven.'

So Merry Hildo married Papa Bois' daughter but he never told anyone except his mother who his wife really was. Hildo himself never hunted again. He and his wife joined forces to run a hospital service for animals.

8. Fairymaids and Mermaids

Stories about mermaids are told in many countries but in the Caribbean there are also stories about fairymaids, the female of the species. As with many of the other supernatural creatures, names may vary from island to island and country to country.

In Grenada there is a large freshwater lake in the crater of an old volcano. It is called the Grand Étang and it is said to be inhabited by a 'Merry Maid', a being which is part human and part fish. Every year people who live in villages near the lake hold a feast and take offerings of every kind of fruit and meat found on the island to the Merry Maid. In return she keeps the lake filled with fresh rain water which the villagers use for watering their terraced farms on the mountains.

In Trinidad, a similar creature known as

103

Mama De l'eau (Mama Dlo) lives in rivers and in the seas around the island. She is sometimes seen sitting on a rock combing her long silken hair with a jewel-studded comb. People say that anyone who finds this comb may enjoy good fortune. These water-beings are fallen spirits and the fairymaids may have one human leg with a cloven hoof like La Diablesse. Sometimes fairymaids and mermaids fall in love with human beings ...

There was once a young woman called Margaret who was so beautiful that her fame spread to every county in the island of Tobago and many songs were composed about her. Margaret was also an excellent swimmer, equally at home in river and sea.

She was swimming in the sea one day when a man suddenly appeared beside her. He was young and handsome and soon they were chatting like two old friends. After a while the man said to Margaret, 'There are some lovely underwater gardens not far from here but you would have to be a strong swimmer to get there. Are you a good swimmer, Margaret?'

Margaret was taken aback when he spoke her name for she had not told it to him. However, she replied, 'I have been told that I'm like a fish in water.'

'You have no fear of the sea then?' he enquired.

'I fear the sea as much as I fear the land. No more, no less.' said Margaret.

'Right then, let us see what kind of fish you are,' he said. And seizing her hand he dived so swiftly that before she knew it she was in a large hall with walls of coral, festooned with sea-green vines. The rooms which led off from the hall were a sight to behold and were paved with marble floors that shone like glass.

There Margaret saw her companion fully for the first time and realised that he was no mortal man but a mermaid. She was not afraid of him for he continued to treat her with the utmost courtesy. She herself had an open curiosity about everything and was fascinated by the spectacular undersea gardens which the

105

mermaid showed her. There was so much to see that Margaret was surprised when he said to her, 'You have been with us for three days. Would you like to stay and be my true companion, Margaret?'

'Three days! Why, I thought I had been here only a few hours. How is it that I have neither eaten nor slept and I feel none the worse for it?' asked Margaret. 'Time feels different here because there is no change of light and also because of the flow of water. But tell me Margaret, will you stay?'

Margaret did not know what to do or say. To tell the truth she was in love with this gentle man of the sea who treated her like a princess. But to stay with him meant that she would never see her folk and friends again. She was clever enough not to provoke his anger with a hasty refusal so she said, 'Let me think about it for a little longer.'

Now that she knew he wanted her to stay Margaret was careful about what she consumed. She had once been told that these beings could bewitch a person by giving them certain things to eat and drink. So she drank only clear water and ate only sea-grapes. Finally she told the mermaid that she wished to return to her world. 'I am likely to die from homesickness if I stay with you,' she said. And since he loved her truly he let her go and took her up through what seemed to be a special tunnel to the beach nearest her village. But before they parted he gave her a beautiful stone which reflected the colours of the rainbow when it was held up to the sun.

'It will ensure a long and full life, and good fortune will be with you always,' said the mermaid when he gave it to her.

And so it was. She lived to be over one hundred

106

years old and she never lost her beauty. She never moved from her village near the sea and asked to be buried at sea when she died.

Strange Journey

Long long ago when people travelled by horse and pony a doctor was on his way home from visiting one of his patients. The moon was full and bright and the doctor decided to take the beach road home. As he rode along he saw a strange shape at the edge of the water. At the same time his horse reared up and threw him to the ground.

When he got up and dusted himself off, he looked closely at the figure and saw that it had a man's body from the waist up and the body of a fish from the waist downwards.

'As I live and die, a mermaid!' exclaimed the doctor. 'I can hardly believe my eyes.'

'Forgive me for disturbing you but I beg you to come with me,' said the mermaid. Needless to say the doctor was quite taken aback at this request. He knew well what the mermaid was asking for he had been brought up on local lore about sea creatures inviting human beings to their underwater home. Nevertheless he wanted to know what the mermaid had in mind for him.

'I'm sure that you have a reason for wanting me to go below with you but I must know what it is,' said the doctor.

'My wife is seriously ill and we have done all we can yet she does not respond. I believe that you can help her.'

Well, the doctor was a man who put his professional duty above personal safety. Without further hesitation he unstrapped his medical bag from the horse and said to the mermaid, 'Now you must find a way to get me and my medicine chest to your home in safety. But remember that I am a poor swimmer.'

The mermaid made a sign to the doctor to follow him and led the way along the beach to a tubular object made of sealskin. He told the doctor to enter the tube which was closed at one end. When the doctor was inside the mermaid closed and secured the flap at the other end. Then he dived with it under the water. Before the doctor could think of what might befall him, the flap was opened and the mermaid was helping him from the tube. He stepped out on to a courtyard covered with black sandy soil, which stuck to his shoes.

He was taken through a door and ushered into a large room where a beautiful woman lay on a bed of seaweed. The doctor was surprised to see that she was a human being and realised that it was the reason he had been sought out. He examined the woman and found that she was burning up with fever and was delirious.

'How long has she been like this?' asked the doctor.

'The reflection of the moon has come into the water three times and three times it has gone away.'

The doctor wasted no time. If for the last three nights the woman's temperature was as high as it was on that night he knew he would have to work fast or she would be past help. Fortunately he had with him medicine which could reduce a temperature quickly and he gave her a strong dose of it. He knew that if the woman died his own life might be forfeit but he tried to appear calm and assured the mermaid that the medicine would soon begin to act and the woman would be cured in a matter of hours.

The mermaid said to him, 'You must stay with us until my wife recovers but do not worry, you will be rewarded for your services.'

While they waited the mermaid called to someone to bring the doctor some refreshment but he never left his side. Anyway it was clear to the doctor that he would not be able to escape without the mermaid's help. All he could do was to pray that the woman recovered.

He must have dozed off for the next thing he knew, the mermaid was shaking him and pointing to the bed where the woman lay. The doctor saw that she was sitting up and talking quite sensibly. 'Oh, I'm so hungry. Do bring me something to eat.'

'Give her something cool and refreshing first,' said the doctor. 'She will have a terrible thirst after her fever.'

He made sure that her temperature was normal but left some of the medicine with the mermaid with instructions about how much should be taken at any one time. Then the mermaid took him back to the surface the same way he had been taken below the water, and set him safely on shore.

Early next morning, the doctor's wife saw a sack outside the front door and opened it. It was filled with gold and silver coins. On the sack was black sand just like the sand on the shoes the doctor had worn on the previous night when he made the strange journey!

Nothing but a pair of shoes

The waters of the island of Tobago are said to be the home of fairymaids and mermaids. In one of the villages there lived a boy called Thomasos. Even as a baby he loved the water and long before he could walk he used to crawl down to the river and peer through the water at the fish swimming on the river bed.

Thomasos grew into an open, good-natured youth but in his eighteenth year a change came over him. Nothing seemed to interest him but the river. He became secretive and hardly spoke to anyone. He refused to go out with his friends and one by one they left him alone. All but a girl named Rosa who had loved Thomasos since they were children.

Rosa was sure that Thomasos was in love with a girl from another village so she began to spy on him. One evening she followed him as he went down to the edge of the river. She saw him sit down on a boulder, remove his shoes and roll up his trouser legs. Rosa settled herself behind a hedge of hibiscus and waited to see what would happen.

The sun was sinking slowly on the horizon, leaving a trail of gold and orange and red bands in the sky. There was a sudden ripple of water and a head emerged from the middle of the river. It was a woman whose hair fell in thick tresses to her waist. It gleamed blue in the glow of the setting sun. From where Rosa was hiding the woman seemed to be gliding in the water and when she drew near the bank, Thomasos waded into the water to meet her. They embraced and, arm in arm, headed towards the boulder.

Rosa's senses were reeling. Then she saw something

else. Thomasos's friend was a fairymaid – a being part woman, part fish – and considered by humans to be a creature of the worst kind.

Rosa ran as fast as her legs could carry her to Thomasos's house. When she arrived she was in such a state that all she could do was to rock back and forth in uncontrollable spasms and repeat over and over, 'Lost, Thomasos is lost, O my God, lost. He is lost.'

'Rosa, child, tell us what is the matter?' asked Thomasos's mother. But it was some time before Rosa was calm enough to speak.

'Thomasos is in love with a fairymaid. I just see them together down by the river,' she said at last, still sobbing loudly.

The mother ran to the windows and shut and latched them. Then she whispered, 'For the love of God, Rosa, don't speak so loud. You sure this is truth?'

'Yes, yes I see it all from the hedge by the river bank. Come and see for yourself if you don't believe me,' said Rosa.

It was a bitter truth for Thomasos's parents to accept but they did not really doubt Rosa's story. Her distress was too genuine and besides both parents had sensed that something was troubling Thomasos.

'That boy been acting strange for a long time but I never thought to see the day when such a thing could happen to my child,' said the father shaking his head.

'But what will you do to help Thomasos?' asked Rosa.

'Listen now, Rosa, you keep silent about what you see tonight down by the river or your life will be in danger. We will try and get help for Thomasos,' said the father.

111

On the following day Thomasos's father paid a visit to a man in the neighbouring village. This man was known as John the Workman because he was well versed in secret rituals of the supernatural. Two days later John the Workman in the guise of a labourer came to the village where Thomasos lived. He offered to do odd jobs such as mending roofs and repairing nets during the day. But at night his business was quite different. He found the place where Rosa was hiding when first she saw the fairymaid and Thomasos. The hedge was high up on the bank of the river but close enough for John to see what took place.

After a few nights of waiting and watching, John went to see the parents of Thomasos to tell them what he knew and what had to be done.

'There is still hope for the boy,' he said, 'for although his shadow is faint it is still with him. The moment you cannot see his shadow the fairymaid will have got him body and soul.'

Then Thomasos's mother wept and his father asked, 'What can you do to save our son?'

'What I have in mind will be dangerous for Thomasos and difficult for you to bear,' replied John.

'We will do whatever you think best,' said the father at once, and the mother nodded her head for her heart was too heavy for words.

'First, you must warn Thomasos that if he does not break with the creature he will lose his soul. When you have done that we will make more plans,' said John.

When Thomasos returned home that evening his mother told him all she knew. He neither admitted nor denied her accusation but remained silent. She fell on her knees and prayed to her dead mother, 'O Ma, help your grandson Thomasos, I beg you. For the love you bore him when you were alive, return and protect him from this danger.'

At this point Thomasos broke down and wept for he cherished the memory of his grandmother. 'Help me, granma. I am too weak to help myself,' he cried. And he told his mother how in the beginning he had tried to break the friendship with the fairymaid but failed. 'Her will is stronger than my fear of being damned,' he said to his mother. But when his mother told him about John the Workman and the help that he could give him, Thomasos agreed to try and do whatever John advised.

On that same night Thomasos and John went down to the river. In his hand John carried a stick with carvings on it. Thomasos wore a new pair of shoes. It had been difficult for John to persuade the parents to remain at home but they agreed because they trusted him. He had explained to them how much the fairymaid wished to make Thomasos her partner and have him live in her world. Once the sea-creatures set their hearts on human lovers they would rather see them dead than lose them.

As the moon rose over the river, the fairymaid appeared and glided through the water to the place where Thomasos sat on the boulder. John was hidden behind it. At the sight of the fairymaid Thomasos forgot his promise to John and tried to go to meet her but the Workman was prepared. He gripped Thomasos's legs firmly to restrain him. The fairymaid wondered at her lover's stillness yet she came gliding on, and, when she was near, Thomasos stretched out his arms to hold her.

Instantly John was out of his hiding-place and had grabbed the thick tresses of the fairymaid which he

113

wound around the stick he carried. He dragged her to the bank but she threw a comb to Thomasos and shouted, 'Throw it into the river, Thomasos.'

'No! No!' commanded John the Workman. 'Give me the comb.'

'If you love me, Thomasos, throw it into the river,' she pleaded.

Thomasos could not help himself. Her power over him was too strong. He threw the comb into the river and immediately he did so, the fairymaid changed into a cat, sprang from the Workman's grasp and leapt into the river.

'O Thomasos!' cried the Workman. 'You have made our task much harder tonight because you disobeyed

114

me. There is only one thing to do now. You must call her up from the river.'

Thomasos looked at the Workman in surprise. 'But after what has happened surely she will not come again?' he exclaimed.

'Oh, yes, she will come again, my boy but only you can call her up,' replied John.

'Tell me what to do now,' said Thomasos.

'If you had followed my instructions she might have agreed to free you from her spell because of the love you shared. But now she is angry and she will be brooding over what happened. She knows that it will never be the same between you after tonight, and fairy-maids are bad losers, Thomasos. You must promise on your grandmother's memory to follow my advice.'

Thomasos said, 'My grandmother's spirit will be with me.'

Then the Workman gave him a secret word and he told him what to do. He stayed close to Thomasos but he did not touch him nor could he interfere until Thomasos had done his part.

Thomasos said the word and the waters parted and the fairymaid appeared. She came near enough to the bank so that Thomasos could see her beauty but this time she stayed out of reach.

Then she stretched out her arms and cried, 'Thomasos, if you cannot accept my love any more at least give me one last kiss that I may remember our love!'

Thomasos was so touched at her despair that he would have risen to go to her but just then he heard the cry of a cat in the distance and he remembered what had taken place earlier that night. He turned away from her.

And now he was joined by John the Workman who

115

had been standing a little way off. John asked the fairymaid, 'What payment will you take to free this mortal?' She was no longer beautiful and soft-spoken. Her face was ugly with malice and her voice harsh with hate. 'Nothing that you can offer me will pay for the love you have destroyed. I would rather have him dead!' she screamed.

'Perhaps so,' replied John the Workman calmly. 'But I have in my hand something of yours which will weaken your power if you harm him.' And opening his hand he revealed three strands of her hair.

She gave a hiss of surprise as she gazed at the strands of hair, and for what seemed an eternity to Thomasos, her eyes were locked with those of the Workman's as if in a silent struggle for mastery.

Suddenly she asked, 'What will you give me to free him?'

'Nothing but a pair of his shoes and three strands of hair,' replied John.

And so it was that as the moon was catching day, Thomasos was set free from his bewitchment by a fairymaid.

Do you know that he never wore shoes after that night. After all it was *his* pair of shoes that the fairymaid took and who knows what she might do to a pair of shoes to draw him back to her!

Mister Noel

Once upon a time many people believed that to fish during Holy Week was to invite the hostility of the spirits of river and sea. Perhaps there are some who still hold that belief. Whether so or not, Mister Noel was not one of them and no one could persuade him to leave off fishing in that particular week.

'If it's safe to eat fish on Good Friday then it's safe to catch fish in the week of Good Friday,' replied Mister Noel when he was warned about the fishing. And off he went to the river to set his nets and traps.

From Sunday to Wednesday of Holy Week he caught many different kinds of fish. He caught so much that for once his basket was filled to overflowing. On Thursday he set out for his village carrying on his head the basket brim-full of fish. He had not travelled half a mile from the river when he heard a strange sound behind him. He looked back. What he saw filled him with such horror that he stopped dead in his tracks.

An enormous white horse was galloping through the woods with a creature, half woman, half serpent, perched on its back. Her tawny long tresses streamed out behind her as she urged the horse onwards with her serpent-like tale.

'Tonné! C'est Mama Dlo!' cried Mister Noel and he took to his heels. But no matter how fast he ran he heard the clip-clop of the horse's hooves and the slip-slap of the serpent's tail on the horse's shanks and his heart felt fit to burst. He knew the basket of fish was holding him back for it was heavy but Mister Noel could not bear to lose *all* his fish. Besides, he knew how his friends would gloat over his misfortune. So he threw out a third of the fish to lighten the load.

When Mama Dlo saw him do this she called out,

'Fish or no fish I go catch you man,
Fish or no fish I go whup you man,

117

You come in me water,
Me children you slaughter
Every week in the year.
You too greedy man!'

And with that the horse made a spurt which narrowed the distance between man and beast. Mr Noel heard the threat and soon felt the hot breath of the horse close behind. Suddenly Mister Noel saw they were coming to another river. He did not dally any longer with the basket of fish but threw all his remaining catch – and the last of his pride – to the winds and plunged into the water just ahead of the horse. Mama Dlo could not enter any other river but her own. As he swam across the wide wide stream she called out to him from the bank, 'Ho! Man, you get away from me but you better watch out because there's a Mama just like me in the river you're in now!'

Mister Noel was still in danger. A serpent woman of any river could smell a human being very quickly, especially if that human carried the taint of fish. With the warning of Mama Dlo ringing in his head Mister Noel strained every muscle to reach the safety of the far side before he was caught.

He was within leaping distance of the other bank when he heard a whistling sound and he felt a stinging lash across his back. Whack! Even through his oilskin jerkin the blow was so powerful that Mister Noel shot out of the water like a flying fish and landed on the river's edge. He was bent double with pain from the whiplash of the second Mama's tail. Another lash would have cut him in half; but she could come no further for at Mister Noel's back was a small village church with a cross rising above the door.

118

As soon as Mister Noel could stand he went into the church to say a prayer of thanksgiving for his life. Then he walked home slowly, thinking about the strangeness of the world and the creatures in it. And since that day no one can persuade Mister Noel to go fishing in river or in sea at any time of the year.

Anita Desai

THE PEACOCK GARDEN

1947 and a new country – Pakistan – has just been created. That long hot summer was a time of terror for the many Muslims of the Punjab, who fled in their thousands to an unknown future in Pakistan.

This is the story of Zuni, a Muslim girl, whose family sought refuge in their local mosque, rather than leave their homeland. Living in the secrecy of the mosque gardens, Zuni is enraptured by the brightly coloured peacocks who also live there but she is also lonely – even though her Hindu friends are just on the other side of the wall.

A moving tale from a distinguished writer.

Jamila Gavin

I WANT TO BE AN ANGEL

Four children, each with a dream:

Effie, who desperately wants to be an angel in the school nativity play, and even more desperately wants to keep her family together . . .

Rajiv, miserable because his sister has gone back to India, but who is happy to find real friendship instead . . .

Dawlish Dobson who is always helpful, but Edward is not so sure that he wants him as a friend – what is Dawlish hiding?

Jasmine just wants a family to call her own, and a friend to play with . . .

Jamila Gavin writes with warmth and sympathy about children who belong to two different cultures.

Jamila Gavin

THREE INDIAN PRINCESSES

The stories of Savitri, Damayanti and Sita

★ *Savitri* ★

Savitri leaves the palace to live with her husband in the jungle. She carries a dark secret. Satyvan will die within a year . . .

★ *Damayanti* ★

Everyone wishes to marry Princess Damayanti, even the gods. However, even the gods consent to the virtuous princess's marriage to King Nala . . . that is all except a demon who lays a curse on the couple.

★ *Sita* ★

Prince Rama is about to become king when he is banished by his jealous stepmother for 14 years. His wife, the loyal Sita, follows, but this is only the beginning of their suffering . . .

Three vibrant and powerful Indian folk-tales retold with great sensitivity and charm.

Geraldine Kaye

COMFORT HERSELF

Comfort loved her mum; everybody loved Margaret. When the tragedy struck it was impossible to believe. But Comfort was on her own now.

'You have to stand up for yourself,' Margaret had said. And Comfort knew she had a choice. She could stay safe in England with her old-fashioned grandparents – or she could try and go to her father in Ghana. It was a hard choice to make, and one she would have to go on making, in one way or another, for the rest of her life.

GREAT COMFORT, the sequel to COMFORT HERSELF, is also available from Mammoth.

Penelope Lively

UNINVITED GHOSTS

What would you do if a ghost not only sat in your room every night knitting, but also asked its friends and relations along as well? Or if a Martian got stranded in your back garden? Or if you wished you could have this all over again – and your wish came true?

All kinds of strange things can happen to perfectly ordinary people – and they *do*, in these ingenious and funny tales, with a surprise at every turn.

A collection of intriguing and witty stories by the author of the Carnegie-winning *The Ghost of Thomas Kempe*.

'All the authentic Lively qualities, of engagement, fun, observation . . . a book to cherish, to read again and again, and to lend to others at your peril – they'll never give it back.'
Junior Bookshelf

Alison Prince

THE GHOST WITHIN

A ghostly trumpet . . . a lost photograph of a lost
lover . . . blood on a dressmaker's pin . . . flowers
of the dead . . .

Alison Prince has created a haunting collection of
stories with the power to startle, disturb and alarm;
they linger long afterwards in the shadowy corners
of your mind.

A Selected List of Fiction from Mammoth

While every effort is made to keep prices low, it is sometimes necessary to increase prices at short notice. Mandarin Paperbacks reserves the right to show new retail prices on covers which may differ from those previously advertised in the text or elsewhere.

The prices shown below were correct at the time of going to press.

☐	7497 0978 2	**Trial of Anna Cotman**	Vivien Alcock	£2.50
☐	7497 0712 7	**Under the Enchanter**	Nina Beachcroft	£2.50
☐	7497 0106 4	**Rescuing Gloria**	Gillian Cross	£2.50
☐	7497 0035 1	**The Animals of Farthing Wood**	Colin Dann	£3.50
☐	7497 0613 9	**The Cuckoo Plant**	Adam Ford	£3.50
☐	7497 0443 8	**Fast From the Gate**	Michael Hardcastle	£1.99
☐	7497 0136 6	**I Am David**	Anne Holm	£2.99
☐	7497 0295 8	**First Term**	Mary Hooper	£2.99
☐	7497 0033 5	**Lives of Christopher Chant**	Diana Wynne Jones	£2.99
☐	7497 0601 5	**The Revenge of Samuel Stokes**	Penelope Lively	£2.99
☐	7497 0344 X	**The Haunting**	Margaret Mahy	£2.99
☐	7497 0537 X	**Why The Whales Came**	Michael Morpurgo	£2.99
☐	7497 0831 X	**The Snow Spider**	Jenny Nimmo	£2.99
☐	7497 0992 8	**My Friend Flicka**	Mary O'Hara	£2.99
☐	7497 0525 6	**The Message**	Judith O'Neill	£2.99
☐	7497 0410 1	**Space Demons**	Gillian Rubinstein	£2.50
☐	7497 0151 X	**The Flawed Glass**	Ian Strachan	£2.99

All these books are available at your bookshop or newsagent, or can be ordered direct from the publisher. Just tick the titles you want and fill in the form below.

Mandarin Paperbacks, Cash Sales Department, PO Box 11, Falmouth, Cornwall TR10 9EN.

Please send cheque or postal order, no currency, for purchase price quoted and allow the following for postage and packing:

UK including BFPO
£1.00 for the first book, 50p for the second and 30p for each additional book ordered to a maximum charge of £3.00.

Overseas including Eire
£2 for the first book, £1.00 for the second and 50p for each additional book thereafter.

NAME (Block letters) ....

ADDRESS ....

....

☐ I enclose my remittance for ....

☐ I wish to pay by Access/Visa Card Number

Expiry Date